THE STORY BAG

The Story Bag

A Collection of Korean Folk Tales

by KIM SO-UN
translated by Setsu Higashi
illustrated by Kim Eui-hwan

CHARLES E. TUTTLE CO.
Rutland, Vermont
Tokyo, Japan

Representatives

For Continental Europe:
BOXERBOOKS, INC., Zurich

For the British Isles:
PRENTICE-HALL INTERNATIONAL, INC., London

For Canada:
HURTIG PUBLISHERS, Edmonton

For Australasia:
BOOK WISE (AUSTRALIA) PTY. LTD.
104-108 Sussex Street, Sydney 2000

Published by the Charles E. Tuttle Company, Inc.
of Rutland, Vermont and Tokyo, Japan
with editorial offices at Suido 1-chome, 2-6
Bunkyo-ku, Tokyo

The stories in this collection originally
appeared in NEGI O UETA HITO,
published in Japanese, 1953, by Iwanami
Shoten, Tokyo

First edition, January 1955
Eleventh printing, 1978

International Standard Book No. 0-8048-0548-2
Printed in Japan

Author's Foreword

I am not yet of an age to be called an old man. But when I compare the world of today with that of my youth, the changes are so great that I can hardly believe they have actually taken place.

When Art Smith, an American, brought the first airplane to Korea, I went, as did other small Korean children, to see the wonderful machine that flew through the skies. With the others, I paid my fifteen sen for admission to the filled-in plot of land in Pusan. There, Art Smith, with his mother in the spare cockpit, put his small one-winged plane into the air, flew daring loops, and wrote his name in smoke across the sky.

Since then only thirty-odd years have passed. Today no Korean child, unless he lives in the most remote mountain fastness, is astonished at airplanes.

♥

In fact, any young schoolboy of the cities can tell the type of plane in flight just by listening, from inside his house, to the sound of the engine. Today, with no trouble at all, one can fly in two or three days to either Europe or the United States. Just last year I myself flew on a 54-passenger SAS passenger air liner to Europe.

Just think—only thirty years ago I watched with beating heart and bated breath a small two-seater doing simple tricks in the air. How the world has changed!

It is not only airplanes that have changed. The way people think and the way they live have also changed. If people who lived even fifty or a hundred years ago were to come back to life, how amazed they would be!

Too frequently our lives undergo change. The world is ever progressing, with neither rest nor pause. Like river rapids, the life of mankind flows forward, day and night, at a dizzying speed, onward and ever onward. This is the ever-changing current of history. But this does not mean that all things change. The beauty of the stars that twinkle in the night sky, the illusive scent of the wild chrysanthemum, the sorrow of parting, the joy of a lovers' reunion, and the nostalgic recollection of a distant journey—these things will remain unchanged forever.

No matter how man's knowledge and wisdom may progress, his inner heart will remain as it was hundreds of years ago. Even if the day should come when man can journey to the moon, as long as man remains man, he will not lose that soul which has been his heritage from time immemorial.

I have chosen and retold here a number of Korean folk tales that have been handed down by word of mouth from one generation to the next. There are stories that have been told by grandparents to their grandchildren, huddled on the heated floors of Korean homes in the dead of winter, with the cold snow-laden winds raging outside. There are stories repeated in the yards of Korean homes to children seated on straw mats in the cool of a summer evening, smoke from mosquito smudges whirling about their faces. These are short tales recounted in great mirth by farmer folk, as they rest from their work in the fields in the shade of a nearby tree. These are stories which the Korean children of countless generations have wept and laughed over in untiring repetition. In these stories tigers smoke tobacco, a tree fathers a child, fleas and lice drink rice-wine, and the spirits of old tales turn themselves into the wild berries of the fields or into a bubbling roadside spring. They reflect the serenity of the men and women nurtured by the ancient land of Korea.

Here may be found stories which echo those told in many other countries throughout the world. Here are also stories that are peculiar to Korea. But you will find here neither homily nor dialectic. I am certain that the reader will feel a kindred spirit with the hearts of the people of ancient Korea. I am certain that a responsive chord will sound in his own heart to their dreams, their laughter, their fantasies.

As seen in the title piece, stories do not like to be hoarded, but want to be told and told again, passing always from lip to lip. These stories were first heard in my childhood in Korean, then written down by me in Japanese, and finally translated into English by Mrs. Higashi. But I have reason to hope that, out of gratitude for the wider audience they can now find, they will use their magic powers to rise above all language barriers and speak directly to the hearts of people in other lands.

Tokyo, Japan   Kim So-un
November, 1954

Contents

THE STORY BAG

1   The Story Bag

 THERE once lived a very rich family. They had only one child, a boy, who loved to have stories told to him. Whenever he met a new person, he would say: "Tell me another different story."

And, each time, he would store away the story he heard in a small bag he carried at his belt. So many stories did he hear that soon the bag was packed tight and he had to push hard to get each new story in. Then, to make sure that none of the stories escaped, he kept the bag tied tightly at the mouth.

The boy eventually grew into a handsome young man. The time came for him to take a wife. A bride was chosen for him, and the whole house was preparing to greet the young master's new wife. Everything was in an uproar.

Now, there happened to be in this rich home a faithful old servant who had been with the family ever since the time when the story-loving boy was still very young. As the household made ready for the young master's wedding, this servant was tending a fire on the kitchen hearth. Suddenly his ears caught faint whispering sounds coming from somewhere. He listened carefully and soon discovered that the voices were coming from a bag hanging on the wall. It was the bag of stories which the young master had kept in his childhood. Now it hung forgotten on an old nail on the kitchen wall. The old servant listened carefully.

"Listen, everyone," said a voice, "the boy's wedding is to take place tomorrow. He has kept us this long while stuffed in this bag, packed so closely and uncomfortably together. We have suffered for a long time. We must make him pay for this some way or another."

"Yes," said another voice, "I have been thinking the same thing. Tomorrow the young man will leave by horse to bring home his bride. I shall change into bright red berries, ripening by the roadside. There

I shall wait for him. I shall be poisonous but shall look so beautiful that he will want to eat me. If he does, I shall kill him."

"And, if he doesn't die after eating the berries," piped up a third voice, "I shall become a clear, bubbling spring by the roadside. I shall have a beautiful gourd dipper floating in me. When he sees me he will feel thirsty and will drink me. When I get inside of him, I shall make him suffer terribly."

A fourth voice then broke in: "If you fail, then I shall become an iron skewer, heated red-hot, and I shall hide in the bag of chaff that will be placed by his horse for him to dismount on when he reaches his bride's home. And when he steps on me, I shall burn his feet badly." Because, you see, according to the custom of the land in those days, a bag of chaff was always placed by the bridegroom's horse so that

he would not have to step directly on the ground.

Then a fifth voice whispered: "If that fails too, I shall become those poisonous string-snakes, thin as threads. Then I shall hide in the bridal chamber. When the bride and the bridegroom have gone to sleep, I shall come out and bite them."

The servant was filled with alarm by what he heard. "This is terrible," he told himself. "I must not let any harm come to the young master. When he leaves the house tomorrow, I must take the bridle and lead the horse myself."

Early next morning, the final preparations were completed, and the wedding procession was ready to set forth. The groom, dressed in his best, came out of the house and mounted his horse. Suddenly the faithful servant came running out and grabbed the horse's bridle. He then asked to be allowed to lead the horse.

The old master of the house said: "You have other work to do. You had better stay behind."

"But I *must* lead the horse today," the servant said. "I don't care what happens, but I insist that I take the bridle."

He refused to listen to anyone and, finally, the master, surprised at the old man's obstinacy, allowed him to lead the horse to the bride's home.

As the procession wound along its way, the bridegroom came to an open field. There by the roadside many bright berries were growing. They looked temptingly delicious.

"Wait!" the bridegroom called out. "Stop the horse and pick me some of those berries."

However, the servant would not stop. In fact, he

purposely made the horse hurry on and said: "Oh, those berries. You can find them anywhere. Just be a little patient. I shall pick some for you later." And he gave the horse a good crack of the whip.

After a while, they came to a bubbling spring. Its clear waters seemed cool and tempting. There was even a small gourd dipper floating on the water, as if to invite the passerby to have a drink.

"Bring me some of that water," the bridegroom said to the servant. "I have been thirsty for some time."

But, again, the servant prodded the horse and hurried by. "Once we get into the shade of those trees, your thirst will soon disappear," he said, and he gave the horse another crack of the whip, a blow much harder than the first.

The bridegroom grumbled and mumbled from atop his horse. He was in a bad mood, but the servant took no notice. He only made the horse hurry the faster.

Soon they reached the bride's home. There, already gathered in the yard, was a large crowd of people. The servant led the horse into the compound and stopped it beside the waiting bag of chaff. As the bridegroom put down his foot to dismount, the servant pretended to stumble and shoved the bridegroom to keep him from stepping on the bag.

The bridegroom fell to the straw mats laid out on the ground. He blushed in shame at his clumsy fall. However, he could not scold the servant in front of all the people. So he kept silent and entered the bride's home.

There, the wedding ceremony was held without untoward incident, and the newly-married couple returned to the groom's home.

Soon night fell, and the bride and bridegroom retired to their room. The faithful servant armed himself with a sword and hid himself under the veranda outside the bridal chamber.

As soon as the bride and bridegroom turned out the lights and went to bed, the servant opened the door of the room and leapt inside.

The newly-wed couple were startled beyond description. "Who's there?" they both shouted, jumping out of bed.

"Young master," the servant said, "I shall explain later. Right now, just hurry and get out of the way."

The servant kicked the bedding aside and lifted the mattress. A terrible sight greeted their eyes. There hundreds of string-snakes coiled and writhed in a single ball. The servant slashed at the snakes with the sword in his hand. As he cut some into pieces, they opened their red mouths and darted their black forked tongues at him. Other snakes slithered here and there, trying to escape the servant's flashing sword. The servant whirled here and there like a madman and finally killed every one of the snakes in the room.

Then he let out a great sigh of relief and began: "Young master, this is the story..." And the old servant recounted the whispers that he had heard coming from the old bag on the kitchen wall.

That is why when stories are heard they must never be stored away to become mean and spiteful, but must always be shared with other people. In this way, they are passed from one person to another so that as many people as possible can enjoy them.

2   The Man Who Planted Onions

 THIS story happened in an age before man ever ate onions. In those days people used to eat people. That was because everybody saw everybody else as cows, not as people at all. If you weren't careful, you'd mistake your own father and mother or your brothers and sisters for cows and eat them up. Surely there can be no sadder plight than this—for people not to be able to tell the difference between people and cows.

Once there was a man who made just such a mistake. He ate up his own brother! After a while he realized what he had done, but by then it was too late. There was nothing he could do to make amends.

"Oh, this is terrible, terrible!" he cried. "I hate living in this place!"

So saying, the man left his home and started on a long journey in search of a place where people saw people as people and not as cows.

"Surely, in this wide, wide world there must be a country when men are men and cows are cows. I don't care how long it takes—I must find such a country."

And so he wandered over the world. He travelled deep into the mountains. He journeyed over the sea. But, no matter where he went, he still found that people ate each other. However, the man refused to give up hope and continued his quest.

He saw many an autumn and many a winter.

The man was young when he started out on his travels. Now he was no longer young. He was an old man. He continued his search, growing older and older. At long last, he came to a country which he had never seen nor heard of before.

Although he didn't yet realize it, this was the country he had been looking for all these long, long years. The inhabitans were all living happily together. Cows were cows, and people were people. They were clearly distinguished.

The aged traveller met up with an old man of this country, who greeted him: "Hello! From where are you? And where are you going?"

"I have no definite place in mind," answered the traveller. "I am only searching for a country where people do not eat each other. Do you think there is such a place in this wide world? I have been searching for such a country for many, many years."

"Oh my, you must have had a hard time," said the aged inhabitant. "We used to be like that here too. People used to look like cows to each other and very often brothers ate brothers and sons ate their parents. But that was all before we began eating onions."

"Onions?" The old traveller was greatly

surprised. "What is that again? Onions? What are onions?"

"Come over here and see for yourself. Those green shoots growing out of the ground there are what we call onions."

The old inhabitant kindly led the aged traveller to a field of onions to show him the sprouting shoots. Not only did the inhabitant show the traveller what onions were, but he also taught the aged visitor in detail how onions were grown and how they were prepared for eating.

The old traveller was greatly pleased. He was given some onion seeds, and then he started on his return trip home.

"By just eating some onions, a person will be able to see his neighbors as human beings and not as cows," he kept telling himself over and over again.

He wanted to get home as soon as he could to tell all his own people about his marvellous discovery. The journey home did not seem too long nor difficult.

At long last he reached his homeland. The first thing he did was to plow his garden and plant the precious onion seeds that had been given him. As soon as he finished planting the seeds, he was so happy that he hurried off to visit his old friends, whom he had not seen for many years.

But, no matter whom he met, he was mistaken for a cow. The people gathered about him and tried to catch him.

"No! No! You are wrong. Look at me well. I am your friend. Don't you remember me?" he cried in a loud voice.

But his friends would not listen to him. "My, what a noisy cow!" they said. "This one really is a cow, isn't he? Let's hurry and catch him."

At last, the old traveller was caught and eaten up by his friends that very day.

Soon after this incident, the people began to notice some strange green shoots, the like of which they had never seen before, growing in a corner of the old man's vegetable garden. Someone plucked one of the green shoots and tasted it. It had a strange, but pleasing, smell.

This was the onion that the old traveller had planted. Of course, no one knew what it was. Nonetheless, all the people flocked to the garden to eat the strange shoots that had a queer but pleasant taste.

To everybody's surprise, after eating the green shoots, people no longer saw each other as cows. They saw each other as they were. No longer was it possible for people to mistake each other for cows.

The people suddenly realized what the old traveller had done. But it was too late to thank him for his efforts. They had already eaten him up. Yet, to this very day, the old man's kindness lives on in the gratitude of the people whom he made happy with the onions he planted.

SPROUTS FARMERS MARKET

SAVE $15

WHEN YOU SPEND $100 ON YOUR HEALTHY GROCERIES

VALID 11/15/21–11/21/21

Use promo code 15HOLIDAY21 to redeem this offer on shop.sprouts.com and save on pickup and delivery orders.

Valid 11/15-11/21/21 in-store & on shop.sprouts.com. Qualifying purchase calculated after applying all other coupons and discounts, & excludes amounts for tax, alcohol, postage & gift cards. Not valid on Instacart or for prior purchases. Excludes Chula Vista, CA & Sprouts Express on High St., Phoenix, AZ. No cash redemption unless required by law (@ 1/100¢. Barcode must be presented at time of purchase in-store and coupon surrendered. To use on shop.sprouts.com promo code 15HOLIDAY21 must be applied at time of purchase. Limit one per customer per visit. Cannot be combined with other Sprouts cash-off offers or the Sprouts Employee Discount. Void if duplicated, sold or transferred. Subject to all applicable laws.

8 9 8 9 9 9 9 9 8 0 4 0 9

SPROUTS FARMERS MARKET

SAVE $10

WHEN YOU SPEND $75 ON YOUR HEALTHY GROCERIES

VALID 12/06/21–12/17/21

Use promo code 10HOLIDAY21 to redeem this offer on shop.sprouts.com and save on pickup and delivery orders.

Valid 12/6-12/17/21 in-store & on shop.sprouts.com. Qualifying purchase calculated after applying all other coupons and discounts & excludes amounts for tax, alcohol, postage & gift cards. Not valid on Instacart or for prior purchases. Excludes Chula Vista, CA & Sprouts Express on High St., Phoenix, AZ. No cash redemption unless required by law (@ 1/100¢. Barcode must be presented at time of purchase in-store and coupon surrendered. To use on shop.sprouts.com promo code 10HOLIDAY21 must be applied at time of purchase. Limit one per customer per visit. Cannot be combined with other Sprouts cash-off offers or the Sprouts Employee Discount. Void if duplicated, sold or transferred. Subject to all applicable laws.

8 9 8 9 9 9 9 9 8 0 4 1 0

Let us handle the prep, so you can enjoy a stress-free holiday.

DON'T DELAY, PRE-ORDER TODAY!

Three simple ways to pre-order your holidays meats, meals and party trays!

- ❯ Text HOLIDAY to 777-688**
- ❯ Scan this QR code
- ❯ Visit **sprouts.com/holiday**

Just heat and serve. Allow two hours for reheating.

3 Mountains and Rivers

 MANY, many years ago there lived in the country of Heaven a king and his beautiful daughter. One day this lovely princess lost her favorite ring. It was a beautiful ring, which she loved dearly. Her father, the king, ordered all his people to look for the ring throughout the country. But it was not to be found anywhere.

Meanwhile, the princess wept and wailed over her loss.

The king could not bear to see his daughter so unhappy. To quiet her sobbing, he told her: "We have searched everywhere in the country of Heaven, but the ring cannot be found. It must have dropped to earth. I will send one of my men to search for it there and to hurry and bring it back to you."

So the king ordered one of his retainers to go down to earth, and there to search for the ring the princess had lost.

You must remember that this happened a long, long time ago, when the earth was still young. It was one great stretch of mud. The retainer did not know where to start his search for the ring. But he had to start somewhere. So he began digging into the mud with his hands. He dug here and there, scooping up the dirt into mounds. He ran his fingers over the ground, leaving deep marks in the surface of the earth.

It was not an easy task to find a small ring in all this mass of mud. But, at long last, he found the precious ring.

The princess was overjoyed and once again became her own happy self.

The deep holes which the retainer dug became oceans. The mounds of dirt he left behind became mountains. And the places where he ran his fingers through the earth became rivers.

That is why the earth now has mountains, rivers and seas.

The Pheasant, the Dove, and the Magpie

4

THERE once lived in the same forest a pheasant, a dove, and a magpie. One year the crops failed, and there was nothing for the three of them to eat.

"What shall we do? How can we live through this cold winter? The three talked over their problems and finally decided to call on a mouse who also lived in the same forest. "Surely," they said, "the mouse will have some rice and will share it with us." They decided that the pheasant would go first to see the mouse.

The peasant was always a proud bird and till then had looked down on the lowly mouse. So, when he came to the home of the mouse, he spoke rudely out of habit.

"Hey there!" the pheasant said haughtily, "where are you? This is the great pheasant. Bring me some food."

Mrs. Mouse was in the kitchen at the back of the house, feeding fuel to her kitchen stove. When she heard the disdainful words of the pheasant, she became very angry. She flew out of the kitchen, a red-hot poker in her hand, and began hitting the pheasant on both his cheeks.

"What's the idea of speaking in such a manner when you have come begging for food. Even if we had rice to throw away, we wouldn't give you any."

Rubbing his red and swollen cheeks, the pheasant ran home in great shame. That is why, to this day, the pheasant's cheeks are red.

Next the dove went to the mouse's home. He, too, was a very proud bird and looked down on the mouse.

"Say, you rice thief! I've come for a bit of food," he said in a rude and haughty manner.

Mrs. Mouse became angry again when she heard the dove speak so rudely. She ran out of her kitchen with a poker in her hand and hit the dove a good blow on the top of his head.

Ever since then, the top of a dove's head has always been blue. It is the bruise that was caused by Mrs.

Mouse and her poker.

Lastly, the magpie went to get some food. The magpie knew too well what had happened to his two friends, the pheasant and the dove. He did not want to repeat their mistakes, so he decided to be very, very careful how he spoke.

As soon as he reached the front door of Mr. Mouse's home, he bowed humbly and spoke as politely as possible. "My dear Mr. Mouse," he said, "we have had a very poor harvest and I am in want. Can you not spare me a little food?"

Mr. Mouse came to the front door. "Well, Mr. Magpie, I won't say I shan't give you anything. But aren't you a crony of the pheasant and the dove? If you are, I will certainly have nothing to do with you."

"Oh no, Mr. Mouse," said the magpie, "absolutely not. I've never even heard of them."

"In that case, come in," the mouse said, believing what the magpie told him. The mouse then gave the magpie some rice to take home.

On top of all this, Mrs. Mouse, her good mood restored, said: "Mr. Magpie, you certainly are a refined gentleman. Even your language is different from the rest. You must have had a very good upbringing."

And so, to this day, the magpie is known for his cunning and slyness.

5 A Dog Named Fireball

ONCE there was, in the world above the skies, a land called the Land of Darkness. It was one country of many in that world, just as we have a number of different nations in the world of man.

This Land of Darkness, as its name implies, had no light whatever. It was a country of perpetual night. Day in day out, year in year out, darkness reigned over the land.

The people of this country were quite used to living without lights. By listening to differences in sounds and by feeling their way about, they were able to find what they wanted. The people were, indeed, expert at groping about in the dark. However, to tell the truth, everybody was quite glum and unhappy. They were all sick and tired of the ever-ing blackness.

Their one cry was: "I wish we had some light! How wonderful it would be to have some light! I wish we could have both day and night, and not just night."

Of course, the king of the Land of Darkness also wanted light. "The world of man below has its sun, and its moon. Isn't there, I wonder, a way of getting some light?" This was the thought which continually ran through the king's mind.

Now, in the Land of Darkness there was a great number of dogs. Everybody kept dogs. But, among these, there was one outstanding animal. He was a great, shaggy creature, but enormously strong and very clever.

This brave animal was endowed by nature with a gigantic mouth. Not only was his mouth excep-tionally large, but it had the peculiar quality of being able to stand any kind of heat. The dog could carry hot things in his mouth—even red-hot balls of fire. Of course, in the Land of Darkness there were almost never any balls of fire, but even if there'd been a dozen a day, the dog could have carried them all. That is why the people of the Land of Darkness called him Fireball. And Fireball he was.

That was not all. He had four of the strongest and fastest legs in all the country. His legs were like steel pillars. He could run hundreds and thousands of miles in the twinkling of an eye.

One day the king had an idea. "Yes, that dog could surely run to the world of man, snatch away the sun, and bring it back to the Land of Darkness," the king thought.

The king called all the wise men of his kingdom together and told them of his idea. They listened to the king, and, when he had finished, one and all clapped their hands in approval and praised the wisdom of their ruler.

"That's it!" they said. "That's the only way to bring light to our country. Fireball will certainly succeed. You have really hit upon a wonderful idea."

Everyone was so overjoyed at the king's suggestion that they were completely carried away. They rejoiced as if Fireball had already brought the sun back in his mouth.

The king was happy too to think that he had thought of such a good plan. He ordered that preparations be made at once for Fireball's departure.

Fireball started out bravely on his long, long

journey. It was a very long trip. Even with his fast legs, it would take Fireball two years to reach the sun. But the dog did not stop to rest. He kept on running and running, day after day, month after month. And at last he reached the skies over the earth.

There the bright sun was, shining in the sky. Soon he was right upon it. It was a huge, round ball of fire.

Fireball opened his enormous mouth and sank his teeth deeply into the sun, trying to tear it out of the sky. But it was hot—terribly hot. It was hotter than any fireball he had ever carried in his mouth before.

Fireball succeeded in getting the sun in his mouth, but he could not bear the heat. He felt as if his whole body would melt from the heat of the sun.

"It's no use. The sun is too hot. At this rate, I won't ever be able to tear the sun out of the sky," the dog said to himself. So he gave up and spit the sun out of his mouth. Then, filled with shame, he returned to the Land of Darkness.

When the king saw Fireball come back without the sun, he was very, very disappointed. Then he thought, "If the sun is too hot, then why not have him bring back the moon?"

"Go to the moon and bring it back," he commanded Fireball. "It should not be as hot as the sun." And so, even before Fireball was able to rest from his long trip to the sun, he was ordered to go to the moon.

After a long journey, Fireball again reached the skies over the world of man. There the moon was, hanging from the sky. It shone with a blue-white light. Sure enough, it did not give off any heat.

"This time I shall be able to take back some light," thought Fireball.

He put his big mouth to the moon and took one bite, just as he had done with the sun. But, oh, it was so very, very cold! It was freezing cold, just like a big lump of ice. Fireball did succeed in getting all the moon into his mouth. But he could not bear the cold. It seemed as if his whole body would freeze. So, once more, he had to give up. He spit the moon out and returned despondently to the Land of Darkness.

When the king saw Fireball come back without the moon, he was again very disappointed. But his wish to have light for his country remained unchanged. In fact, the more he thought of the sun and the moon and how difficult it was to get either, the more he wanted to have one or the other of them brought back. Again he called Fireball and ordered him to go get the sun.

Tired as he was, Fireball again set off bravely. But once again he failed. He did succeed in getting the sun into his mouth, but again he could not bear the heat. So once more Fireball came back to the Land of Darkness, empty-mouthed.

The king, sorely disappointed, next ordered Fireball to try for the moon again. But it was the same story. When he got the moon into his mouth, it

was as cold as ever. He could not stand it. That
was how cold the moon was.

Five times, ten times, twenty times, Fireball repeated the same journey. And each time he failed.
And the oftener the dog failed, the stronger became
the king's desire to bring light to his land.

But the sun was too hot, and the moon was too
cold. No matter how brave and how strong Fireball
was, this was one feat that he could not accomplish.

Still the king of the Land of Darkness would
not give up. His desire to get light for his kingdom
had now become a deeply fixed passion in his mind.
He was sure that, no matter if Fireball failed a
hundred times, nay, a thousand times, there would
come a day when the dog would finally succeed.

"Just watch," the king told himself. "One of these
days Fireball will come home with either the sun
or the moon."

So Fireball kept going to the sun and moon by
turns. Many, many years passed. Fireball was no
longer a young dog. He was no longer as strong
and fleet as he once was. But the king of the Land
of Darkness kept ordering the dog to go for the sun
and the moon.

Even to this present day Fireball continues his

distant trips to the skies above the world of man, first to the sun and then to the moon.

The eclipses of the sun and the moon are signs that Fireball, that brave and loyal dog from the Land of Darkness, is still living, still trying. Each time he grabs the sun or the moon in his mouth he is making another attempt to take light back to his king.

And, doubt it not, Fireball will go right on trying, again and again, until eternity. That's the kind of dog he is.

6 The Deer, the Rabbit, and the Toad

ONCE upon a time, a deer, a rabbit, and a toad lived together in one house. One day they held a great feast to celebrate a happy occasion.

The three began arguing over who should be served first. Finally it was decided that the oldest of the three should begin the feast. This started each of the three boasting of his age.

The deer spoke first. "When heaven and earth were first made," he said, "it was I who helped put the stars in the sky. That shows how old I am. I surely must be the oldest here."

The rabbit then spoke up. "It was I who planted the tree that was used to make the ladder for putting the stars in the sky. You see, I am older than Mr.

Deer. So I must be the oldest here."

All this while the toad had sat silent, listening to the boasting of the others. All at once he began to sob quietly.

The deer and the rabbit were surprised and asked: "What's the matter, Mr. Toad?"

With tears running down his cheeks, the toad answered: "Your talk reminded me of my three sons. When they were still young they each planted a tree.

When the trees grew up, my eldest son cut his down and from it made the handle for the hammer used in nailing the stars to the sky. From his tree my second son made the handle of the spade that was used to dig the channel where the Milky Way now flows. My youngest son used his tree to make the handle of the hammer which nailed the sun and the moon to the sky.

"But now, to my great sorrow, all three sons are dead and gone. I couldn't help but cry as I listened to you two arguing about your age."

At this, both the deer and the rabbit had to agree that Mr. Toad was surely the oldest of them all. So it was toad who was given the honor of being served first.

7 Mr. Bedbug's Feast

FATHER Bedbug was about to greet his sixty-first birthday. Now, in the country where Mr. Bedbug lived, it was the custom to celebrate one's sixty-first birthday in a grand manner, since few people lived that long, to say nothing of bedbugs.

Thus, Mr. Bedbug decided to hold a great feast and invited his two close friends, Mr. Flea and Mr. Louse.

Mr. Flea and Mr. Louse were both happy to be invited. They were sure there would be a groaning board, and both were delighted with the prospect of good food and much wine. They started out together in a very happy mood.

But Mr. Flea, like all of his kind, was a very

short-tempered fellow by nature and, as he walked along with Mr. Louse, he became very impatient, for, as you know, Mr. Louse was a very slow walker. Mr. Flea couldn't help taking a few jumps ahead, and then a few more.

Left way behind, Mr. Louse called out: "Say, don't be so impatient! Try not to hurry and jump ahead so quickly."

Mr. Flea felt ashamed and, for a time, held himself back to walk along side by side with Mr. Louse. But Mr. Louse was really slow. Why, sometimes it was even difficult to tell whether he was walking or standing still. You see, Mr. Louse was a calm person, and he was in no great hurry.

Seeing Mr. Louse so composed and quiet, Mr. Flea could not hold his patience any longer and said: "Mr. Louse, you come along afterwards. It irks me to walk so slowly." No sooner had Mr. Flea said this than he jumped ahead and was at Mr. Bedbug's home in no time.

Mr. Bedbug had really prepared a grand feast for his friends. There were many, many dishes and much wine, all laid out on a large table.

Panting from his hurried walk, Mr. Flea called out to Mr. Bedbug, even before he entered the house, saying: "Oh, but I'm thirsty! Please give me some wine."

"Why, yes," said Mr. Bedbug, "do have some of the wine. But, why, in heaven's name, did you hurry so on such a warm day?" He filled a large bowl to the brim with wine and gave it to Mr. Flea.

Mr. Flea gulped the wine down greedily. Then he said: "Ah, at last I feel refreshed. But I would like another bowl, I think."

And so he drank another bowlful of wine.

Mr. Bedbug and Mr. Flea waited for Mr. Louse to arrive. They waited and waited, but there was no sign of him.

At last, Mr. Bedbug stood up and said: "It's quite a distance for Mr. Louse to walk. Maybe I should go out to meet him."

After Mr. Bedbug was gone, Mr. Flea was left all alone. The sight of all that food on the table and all that wine in the bottle began to torment him. He was already slightly drunk from his two bowlfuls of wine, and he simply couldn't resist the temptation. Slowly he reached for the wine bottle and filled his bowl. He drank one bowlful—two bowlfuls—three bowlfuls. Finally he lost count—and suddenly there was not a single drop of wine left in the bottle.

Soon Mr. Bedbug returned with his other guest, Mr. Louse. They found Mr. Flea lying on the floor, dead drunk, snoring away noisily. They also noticed that there was no more wine left.

Poor Mr. Louse—he had come all this distance to the party, and now there was not so much as a drop of wine left for him. Losing his usual composure, he became very angry.

Suddenly he began kicking Mr. Flea in the back, crying: "Wake up, you impudent thing!"

Mr. Flea woke up with a start. But he was still so drunk that he didn't know what was what, nor why. He couldn't even remember what he had done.

"What's the big idea of kicking me in the back?" he shouted angrily at Mr. Louse.

This, of course, was enough to start a big fight between Mr. Flea and Mr. Louse. Each fought in anger, and neither one would give in to the other. The party was quite ruined.

Mr. Bedbug tried to stop them. He tried to push the two apart, crying: "Here, here! Stop this foolish fighting!"

But Mr. Flea and Mr. Louse were locked tightly together. Suddenly they both toppled over, with a great crash. And where should they fall but right on the very top of Mr. Bedbug's fat stomach!

Poor Mr. Bedbug—his stomach has never mended from that fall. It is still flat to this day.

Mr. Louse—he bruised his hip when he fell. And even today, he still has a black bruise on his hip.

And what of Mr. Flea? Even today his face has the red flush it got from all that wine he drank.

8 Why We Have Earthquakes

 THIS story goes back to the beginning of time. One corner of the floor of Heaven began to sag. It seemed as if Heaven itself would topple over and crash. The king of Heaven became greatly alarmed and ordered a huge pillar of red copper to be made.

What he wanted to do was to use this big pillar to bolster up the sagging corner of Heaven. So he had this pillar set up on the ground of Earth below. But the ground was so soft and Heaven so heavy that the whole pillar kept sinking into the earth and was of no use in holding up the sagging corner of Heaven.

The king of Heaven then searched throughout all his land for the strongest man in his kingdom. Finally he found a man who was enormously strong. He sent this man to Earth and told him to hold the huge copper pillar up on his shoulder. Only in this way was the corner of Heaven finally strengthened and the sagging corrected.

And so, as long as the strong man held the pillar up, Heaven was safe. But he could never take his shoulder away, lest Heaven come crashing down.

So, even unto this day, the strong man still supports the copper pillar. But, of course, the pillar and Heaven are heavy, and the weight becomes painful on his shoulder. And so, every once in a while, the strong man must shift the weight from one shoulder to the other. Every time this happens, the ground quivers and quakes with the man's effort. That is why we have earthquakes.

9 The Stupid Noblewoman

ONCE there was a nobleman's wife who was rather stupid.

One day, the father of her daughter's husband passed away, and the noblewoman went to express her sympathies to the bereaved family. When she arrived at the house, she found the whole family and all the relatives gathered together.

"Aigo, aigo!" they were all crying in sorrow, for, you see, in Korea there is no cry of greater sorrow than this.

When the noblewoman saw this weeping, she felt that she too must express sorrow in the same way. So she joined in the wailing too, sobbing, "Aigo, aigo, aigo!" with the best of them.

As she cried she forgot who it was that had passed

away. She was so moved by her own tears that soon she was thinking it was her own husband who had died. "O my husband, my dear, dear husband!" she wailed. "Take me with you!"

The people around her were astonished at first, but soon they burst out in great laughter.

The foolish noblewoman could not understand why the people were laughing, and she continued weeping. Between sobs she said: "My husband, my dear, dear husband, why have you left me? Please take me with you!"

She had repeated this several times when her daughter quietly poked her in the ribs. The noblewoman suddenly realized that she was not at home but was attending the funeral of her daughter's father-in-law. She saw she had made a big mistake and wondered how she could make amends.

Suddenly she turned around and faced the people gathered there and greeted them politely. Hoping to made them feel better after what she had done, she said: "You are all well, I hope. Is there no great change in the family?"

The people looked at her in surprise. "You ask if there is any change. Could there be a greater change than to have the master of the house pass away?" they asked in utter astonishment.

"Oh, yes," the stupid noblewoman answered, "of course. And what sickness did the master die of?"

"A hammer fell off the shelf—" they began.

But, even before they could finish the sentence, the noblewoman, all eager to be polite, exclaimed: "My, how dangerous! And did he hurt himself? Was it a bad accident?"

"Of course he hurt himself. The master died from the injury caused by the falling hammer. What greater accident could there be?"

When she heard this, the stupid noblewoman became very embarrassed. She realized that everything she had said had only made her seem the more foolish. She racked her brains for something to say that would make things right again. Her gaze wandered to the window, and outside she saw a magpie perched on a bough of a persimmon tree.

Smiling her best smile, the noblewoman pointed to the bird and said: "My, how beautiful! Is that your magpie?"

All the people gathered in the house sat for a moment in stunned silence. Then suddenly they broke into uncontrollable gales of laughter, while the noblewoman sat looking more stupid than ever.

10 The Bridegroom's Shopping

AWAY in the country there once lived a long-established family of farmers. There was an only daughter in the family, who had just married. As is the custom in such cases, the bridegroom came to live with his in-laws, for he was to continue the family name.

A few days after the marriage it so happened that the bridegroom had to go to town on some business. As he prepared to leave, his bride asked him: "Will you please buy me a comb in town?"

"Why, of course," he answered, all eager to please his pretty bride.

However, his wife knew that her husband was a very forgetful man. Hadn't her in-laws told her so?

As she was wondering how he could be made to remember, she chanced to look at the sky. There was
a new moon, a thin crescent of pale light, shining
softly in the sky. It was only three days old, and it
looked just like the moon-shaped comb she wanted.

"There," she called to her husband, "look at the
moon. Doesn't it look just like a comb? If you forget what you must buy, just remember to look into
the sky. The moon will remind you that I want a
comb. You *will* remember, won't you?"

This she repeated again and again, and after she
was sure he would remember, she bade him farewell.

The bridegroom was soon in town. He was so
taken up with his business that he completely forgot
about his wife's comb. Several days later, his work
finished, he packed his belongings and prepared to
return home. As he looked around to see if he had
forgotten anything, he happen to look out the window, and there he saw a big, round moon shining
in the sky. Ten days had passed since he had left
home. The moon was no longer a small sliver of
light but a round, laughing globe of silver.

The moon suddenly reminded him of his wife's
parting words. "Oh, I almost forgot," he told himself. "There was something like the moon I had to

buy for my wife. Now, I wonder what it was?'

Try as he might, he could not remember. He knew that it had something to do with the moon— but what? His memory was a blank. "Was it something round like the moon?" he asked himself, "or was it something that shone like the moon?" But not for the life of him could he recall what it was.

"Well," he said at last, "I might as well go to a shop and ask for help."

So the young farmer entered a shop and said: "Good day, Mr. Shopkeeper. Please give me something that looks like the moon, something a woman uses."

The shopkeeper laughed at this strange request. Then he looked around at the goods on his shelf, and his eyes lighted on a small round hand-mirror.

"Oh, I know," the shopkeeper said. "This must be what you want. Look, it's round and looks just like the full moon. You look into it and you can see yourself. A young bride would want it when she pretties herself. I am sure it could be nothing else."

Now, the bridegroom had never seen a mirror before, as they were very rare then. But he thought that surely his wife, the daughter of a rich old farming family, would know what it was. "Yes, this must be what my wife asked me to get," he answered, proud that he could thus get what his wife wanted.

Soon he was back home in the country again. As soon as he entered the house, his wife asked: "Did you remember to do my shopping for me?"

"Yes," he answered. "Here." And he handed her what he had bought.

The bride, expecting to receive a comb, wondered at the strange round object her husband handed her. She peered into the smooth glass. And what should she see there but the reflection of a young woman— and a very pretty woman at that.

"What thing is this!" she cried. "I only asked for a comb, and here you bring home a pretty young woman." The wife turned angrily and ran to her mother.

"Mother, can you imagine anything so silly? I asked my husband to buy me a comb in town, and look what he brought home—a strange young woman!"

"Where? Where is she?" the mother asked, taking the mirror and peering into it.

Of course, the mother saw reflected only the face of a wrinkled old woman. "Why, my child," she said, "what are you talking about? This must be an old relative of ours from a neighboring village."

"No, you are wrong. It's a young woman," the young wife cried.

"No, it's you who are wrong. Look, she's an old, wrinkled woman," the mother retorted angrily.

Thus the two began quarreling.

Just then a small boy came into the room, eating a rice-cake. The boy picked up the mirror and peered into it. There he saw another boy eating a

rice-cake. The boy thought the stranger had taken his.

"Give me back my rice-cake," he shouted, "it's mine!" He threw up his hand to strike the boy. The boy in the mirror also raised his arm. The bewildered child, scared by what he saw, began to cry loudly.

The room was filled with din, the two women arguing away at the top of their voices, and the boy crying his head off.

Just then the grandfather passed by and heard the commotion. Wondering what it was all about, he poked his head in the doorway. "What's going on here? What's the matter?" he asked. Then he caught sight of the boy looking at a round object and crying: "Give me back my rice-cake!" The grandfather flared with anger to think that someone or something should have taken rice-cakes from a small boy.

"Where, where?" he asked. "Show me the thief!" He grabbed the mirror and peered into it. There, staring at him, was a fierce-looking old man, anger written all over his face.

"Why, it's an old man. You ought to be ashamed at your age to jump out and interfere in a quarrel between boys." With these words the grandfather rolled up his sleeves and was about to hit the old man in the mirror.

Suddenly the mirror slipped from his hand and fell to the floor with a loud crash. The grandfather, and the boy, and the two women, and the bridegroom all fell silent and stood staring dumbly at hundreds of pieces of broken glass beneath their feet.

11 The Bad Tiger

IN a great forest there once lived a very bad tiger. Every night he would come out of his lair and steal into a radish patch kept by a poor old woman. There the bad tiger would trample all over the garden, eating the choicest and fattest radishes.

The poor woman came every morning to her radish patch and cried at the damage caused by the bad tiger. But she didn't know what to do, for the tiger was as strong as he was bad. She wondered and wondered how she could stop the tiger from eating her radishes every night. Finally, she hit upon a good plan.

One day, she met the tiger and said: "Mr. Tiger, why do you have to eat radishes all the time? Please come to my house, and I shall make some delicious, nourishing red-bean gruel for you to eat."

The tiger was overjoyed at the prospect of a red-bean gruel, for it was his favorite dish. "Thank you. I shall be over tonight," he said, licking his chops at the thought of the feast.

The old woman hurried home to prepare for the arrival of the bad tiger. First she lit a fire and heated up a large mass of charcoal. She put the glowing coals in a brazier and took the brazier outside to the back of her home.

Then, she floated some red-hot cayenne pepper on the water in her kitchen water jug.

Next, she stuck a large number of needles in the kitchen towel.

She then scattered cow dung all around the kitchen door, and spread a large straw mat, used in drying unhulled rice, out in the yard.

Finally, she brought out an A-frame, used on the back when carrying heavy loads and so-called because it is shaped like the letter "A" turned upside down. She propped the A-frame up against the back fence.

Now everything was ready. The old woman went back to her kitchen and, as though nothing was out of the ordinary, pretended she was preparing the evening dinner.

Soon it was dark, and the bad tiger came sneaking to her house. The old woman heard the tiger outside and said: "Oh, it's you, Mr. Tiger. Please do come in." And she opened the front door, smiling her welcome at the bad tiger.

"My, it's cold tonight, isn't it, Mr. Tiger?" she said. "You won't mind, will you, bringing the charcoal brazier into the house from the back for me?"

"Of course," the bad tiger said, for he was in a good mood thinking of the feast he was about to have.

He went out back and was about to lift the brazier up when he noticed that the charcoal was almost out. "Say, old woman. The charcoal is almost out. There are hardly any red embers left."

The old woman answered from inside the house: "Is that so? Will you blow the embers for me? The charcoal will soon become red."

The bad tiger put his nose to the brazier and puffed and puffed. He blew so hard that some ashes whirled up and dropped into his eyes. The bad tiger hurriedly rubbed his eyes, but the more he rubbed the more they hurt. In pain, the bad tiger cried: "Old woman, old woman! I've got some ashes in my eyes. Help me!"

"My, I'm sorry," she said. "Try washing your eyes

with water. You'll find some in the kitchen jug there."

The tiger did as he was told. But, as you will remember, the old woman had floated some red pepper on the water. The pepper got in both the tiger's eyes, and he was in greater pain than before. He thought he would surely go blind.

"Old woman, old woman!" he called, "my eyes are worse than before. What can I do?" Then, "Ooh! Ooh!" the bad tiger moaned, pressing his eyes with his front paws and stamping his feet in pain.

"Oh, is it that painful? Try wiping them with this kitchen towel."

The bad tiger was in great pain. He grabbed the towel she handed him and began rubbing his eyes frantically. But the needles in the towel pricked his eyes. Now the bad tiger became truly mad with pain.

Suddenly the bad tiger realized how he had been tricked by the old woman. Blindly he tried to run away. But, as soon as he stepped out the kitchen door, he slipped on the cow dung and fell head over heels on the ground.

The straw mat, which the old woman had laid out in the back yard, saw all this and came flying through the air. It quickly wrapped the bad tiger in a tight roll.

Next, the A-frame came trotting out from the back fence and threw the tightly wrapped tiger on its back. Then, without a word, it ran right down to the sea and threw the bad tiger headlong into the waves.

That was the end of the bad tiger. Thereafter the old woman was able to raise her radishes in peace. There was no longer a bad tiger to come and dig up her radish patch.

12 The Three Foolish Brides

THREE foolish brides had been chased out of their husbands' homes and forced to return to their parents. One day they happened to meet.

"Why were you sent home?" one of the three young women asked one of the other foolish brides.

"It was really nothing at all. My mother-in-law asked me to knock the ashes out of her long tobacco pipe. So I took it outside and knocked the stem a couple of times on a round stone. But, to my bad luck, it turned out to be, not a stone, but the bald head of my father-in-law, glinting white in the moonlight."

The second bride was asked the same question.

"I was chased out for nothing at all too. My

mother-in-law asked me to put some fire in the brazier. So I put some hot embers from the stove in a sifter and brought it in. When the woven horsehair bottom of the sifter caught fire and spilled the embers, they said that I was wrong."

The third bride told her story:

"In my case, it was really nothing too. The young master next door kept saying he was cold. I felt sorry for him and let him put his hands in my bosom to warm them up. Just imagine! Don't you think it really unreasonable of them to make that the excuse for sending me home?"

All three foolish brides felt much better after they'd told their stories and received each other's sympathy.

13 The Tiger and the Rabbit

ONCE a hungry old tiger was walking through the woods, looking for something to eat. By chance he came upon a baby rabbit. The old tiger's eyes glistened to see such a juicy morsel.

"I'm going to eat you up," he told the rabbit.

The baby rabbit, though very small, was a clever fellow. He coolly answered: "Just wait, Mr. Tiger. I'm still too young and small to make good eating. I have something much tastier for you. I shall give you some rice cakes. When you toast them over a fire, they are really delicious."

As he said this, the rabbit stealthily picked up eleven small white stones. He showed them to the tiger.

The greedy tiger became very interested. "But," he said, "how do you eat these?"

The rabbit answered: "Here, I'll show you. You toast them over a fire until they are red-hot, and then you eat them in one gulp. I'll go find some firewood so you can have some right away."

The rabbit gathered together some twigs and sticks and started a fire. The tiger put the eleven stones on the fire and watched them toast.

When the stones were getting hot and red, the rabbit said: "Mr. Tiger, wait a while. If you put soy sauce on the cakes, they will taste even more delicious. I shall get some for you. You must wait now and don't eat any while I am gone.... Let's see, there are ten rice cakes, aren't there?" So saying, the baby rabbit skipped into the woods and ran away toward the village.

As the stones reddened with the heat, the tiger began licking his lips in anticipation. He started counting what he thought were rice cakes.

"One, two, three... Why," he said in surprise, "there are eleven cakes, not ten."

He started counting them over again, but, no matter how many times he counted, there was always one too many.

"The baby rabbit said there were ten. If I ate one, he wouldn't know the difference," the tiger said to himself.

So he quickly took the reddest one from the fire, popped it in his mouth, and gulped it down greedily. But, oh, it was hot! so very, very hot! The tiger not only burnt his mouth and tongue, but his stomach as well. He squirmed with pain. He moaned and groaned and rolled all over the ground.

All of which served the old tiger right for being so greedy. It was some time before he could eat anything again.

One day, much later, the tiger met the baby rabbit again.

"Say you, you bad rabbit! What a time you gave me the other day. I'll not let you go *this* time. Now I'll really eat you up." And the tiger's eyes burned with anger.

But the baby rabbit did not look a bit frightened. With a smile he answered: "Don't be so angry, Mr. Tiger. Please listen to me. I have found a way to catch hundreds and thousands of sparrows. All you have to do is to keep perfectly still with your mouth wide open. The sparrows will come flying right into your mouth and make a nice feast for you."

The old tiger licked his lips and asked: "Oh, is that so? What else am I supposed to do?"

"Oh, it isn't difficult at all. All you need do is to look up at the sky and keep your mouth open. I'll chase the sparrows out of the bamboo thicket into your mouth."

Once again the old tiger did as he was told.

The baby rabbit hopped into the bamboo thicket  and set fire to a pile of dry leaves and twigs. The sound made by the burning leaves and twigs was just like the fluttering of thousands of sparrows.

The tiger, meanwhile, kept gazing up at the sky, his mouth wide open. "Why, it does sound as if the birds were flying this way," he thought. And he kept right on staring up at the sky, his mouth wide open, waiting for the sparrows to fly into it.

From a distance, the baby rabbit cried: "Shoo! shoo!" pretending he was chasing sparrows.

"Mr. Tiger, Mr. Tiger, a lot of birds are flying your way now. Don't move! Just wait a while longer."

So saying, the baby rabbit scampered away to safety.

The fire came closer and closer to the tiger, and the noise became louder and louder. The tiger was sure the birds were coming his way, and he patiently waited. Soon the noise was all about him, but not a single sparrow popped into his mouth.

"That's funny," thought the tiger, and he took his eyes from the sky and looked around him. To his surprise, there was one great ocean of fire all about him as far as he could see.

The tiger became frantic with fear as he fought his way through the burning woods. Finally he managed to come through alive, but his fur was all sizzled black. And his skin looked like newly tanned hide.

It was soon winter. Once again the tiger became ravenously hungry. As he stalked through the forest looking for food, he came to the banks of a river. There he saw his old friend, the baby rabbit, eating some vegetables.

The tiger roared angrily at the rabbit: "How dare you fool me about the sparrows! I won't let you get away with anything *this* time. I will eat you up for sure." He ground his teeth and ran up to the rabbit.

The rabbit smiled as usual and said: "Hello, Mr. Tiger, it's quite some time since we last met, isn't it? Look, I was just fishing with my tail in the river. I caught a big one, and it was delicious. Don't you think river fish are very tasty?"

The hungry tiger gulped with hunger and said: "You were fishing with your tail? Show me how it is done."

"It isn't very easy," the rabbit replied, "but I'm sure you will be able to do it. All you need to do is to put your tail in the water and shut your eyes. I shall go up the river a little and chase the fish this way. Remember, you mustn't move. Just wait a little, and you'll have many fish biting at your tail."

The old tiger did what the rabbit told him. He put his tail into the river, closed his eyes, and waited.

The rabbit ran up the river bank and hopped about here and there, pretending to chase the fish down to where the tiger was waiting. The winter day was beginning to wane, and the water became colder and colder.

"The fish are beginning to swim your way, Mr. Tiger," the rabbit shouted. "They will be biting on your tail any minute. Don't move!" Then the rabbit ran away.

The river began to freeze over slowly. The old tiger moved his tail a wee bit. It was heavy. "Ah, good! I must have caught a lot of fish on my tail. Just a while longer and I shall have a good catch," he told himself.

He waited until midnight. "Now I shall have lots of fish to eat," thought the tiger.

So he tried to pull his tail out. But it wouldn't move! What had happened? Why, his tail was frozen tightly in the ice.

"Oh, I have been tricked again by that rabbit," moaned the tiger. But, it was too late to do anything.

When it became light, the villagers came to the river and found the old tiger trapped in the ice. Thus the greedy old tiger was finally caught and taken away. And that was one greedy old tiger who never ate another rabbit.

14   The Great Flood

ONCE upon a time, long, long ago, there lived a handsome boy named Talltree. He was so named because his father was a tree—a tree so tall that it almost reached the sky. His mother was a celestial being, a beautiful creature from Heaven who came down to earth from time to time. She often used to rest in the shade of the tall tree. In time she became the tree's wife and bore a boy child, who became the Talltree of this story.

When Talltree was about to greet his eighth spring, his mother left him beside his father, the great, tall tree, and returned to her home in the heavens.

One day a terrible storm arose suddenly. For days on end the rains poured down on earth, until all the ground was under water. Soon mountainous waves began sweeping toward the tall tree, the father of the young boy.

Father-tree became alarmed. He called to his child and said: "I shall soon be uprooted by this terrible storm. When I fall, you must climb into my branches and perch on my back. Otherwise, you will be drowned."

The storm became more and more violent. Lashed by screaming winds, great waves thundered against the trunk of the tree. Then came the fiercest gust of all, and the kingly tree fell with a crash.

Quickly the boy climbed on his father's back and held tightly to the branches. The great tree floated on the rushing waters. For days and days it drifted on and on, at the mercy of the angry waves.

One day they came upon a great number of ants struggling in the water. The poor ants, on the point of drowning, cried: "Save us! Save us!"

Talltree felt sorry for them and asked his father: "Shall we save the ants?"

"Yes," his father replied.

"Climb up on my father's back," Talltree called to the ants, "and you will be saved. Hurry! Hurry!"

And Talltree helped the tired and weary ants get

up out of the wind-whipped water onto the tree. The
ants, of course, were very happy to be saved.

Soon, a great cloud of mosquitoes came flying
through the storm. They, too, were weary, for nowhere was there any place to land and rest their tired
wings.

"Help! Help!" the mosquitoes buzzed.

Again, Talltree asked: "Father, shall we save the
mosquitoes?"

"Yes," his father replied.

So Talltree helped the tired mosquitoes alight on
the leaves and branches of his father's back. The
mosquitoes were also very grateful to be saved from
the cruel storm.

As Talltree and his father and the ants and the
mosquitoes drifted along, they heard the cry of a child.
They looked into the waves and saw it was a boy
about the same age as Talltree.

"Save me! Save me!" cried the boy.

Talltree felt sorry for the boy. "Let's save the
boy too," he said.

But this time his father didn't answer.

Again the cries of the boy came pitifully across
the raging waters. And again Talltree said: "Please,
Father, let's save that boy."

Still there was no answer from Father-tree.

Talltree pleaded with his father a third time: "Father, we must save that poor boy!"

The father finally answered: "Do as you wish. I leave it up to you."

Talltree was overjoyed and called to the boy to come and climb up onto his father's back. So the boy was saved too.

After a long time, the father-tree, Talltree, the ants, the mosquitoes, and the boy who had been saved from the waves came to an island. It was the peak of the highest mountain in that country—a mountain as high as Paik Tu, the Mountain with a White Head, so called because the snows never melted from its crest.

As soon as the tree reached the island, the ants and the mosquitoes thanked Talltree and took their departure.

The two boys were very hungry, for they had not eaten for many days. They wandered over the island searching for food and finally came upon a small straw-thatched hut.

"Please give us some food," the boys cried out.

An old woman and two young girls came out. They welcomed the boys into the house and gave them food. One of the girls was the real daughter of the old woman and the other an adopted child.

The great flood and storm had destroyed everything on earth except this little island. The only people left in the world were the two boys, the old woman, and the two girls. There was no other place where the boys could stay. So from that day forth they lived with the old woman, working for her as servants.

It was a peaceful life. The days slipped into weeks, the weeks into months, and the months into years, and the boys grew into strong, fine youths.

As the old woman watched the boys grow into manhood, she thought to herself: "They will make fine husbands for my two girls."

One day, she called the two of them to her and said: "Whichever of you is the more skillful shall have my own daughter for his wife, and the other shall have my adopted girl."

Now the old woman's own daughter was the more beautiful of the two girls, and the boy who had been saved by Talltree during the flood wanted very much to marry her. He thought of a way to get her for his own wife.

"Grandma," he said, "Talltree has a strange power which none of the rest of us has. For example, you can mix a whole sack of millet in a pile of sand, and he can have the millet and the sand separated in no time. Let him try it and show you."

The old woman was astounded to hear this. "Is that so?" she said. "I would like very much to see his wonderful ability. Come, Talltree, let me see if you really can do this amazing thing."

Talltree knew he was being tricked. He knew he certainly could do no such thing. He knew the other youth was planning to get him into trouble. So he refused. But the old woman was adamant. She was determined that Talltree should show her his strange power.

"If you don't do it, or if you can't do it, I won't give you my daughter in marriage," the old woman said.

Talltree saw he couldn't escape and sighed. "Very well, then," he said, "I'll try."

The old woman emptied a sack of millet into a pile of sand and mixed them all up together. Then she left, saying she would return in a short while to see how he was getting along.

Talltree gazed hopelessly at the pile of millet and sand. What was he to do? It was not humanly possible to sort the millet from the sand.

Suddenly, Talltree felt something bite his heel. He looked down, and there he saw a large ant.

"What is troubling you, Talltree?" the ant asked. "I suppose you no longer remember me, but I am one of the ants you saved a long time ago in the flood. Tell me, what's the matter?"

Talltree told the ant how he must separate the millet from the sand or else not be able to marry the old woman's daughter.

"Is that all the trouble? Then your worries are over. Just leave it to me."

No sooner had the ant said this than a great mass of ants came swarming from all over the place. They attacked the huge pile of sand and millet, each ant carrying a millet grain in its mouth and putting it into the sack placed nearby. Back and forth the ants hurried. In almost a twinkling of an eye all the millet was back in the sack.

When the old woman came back, she was amazed to find that Talltree had finished an impossible task in so short a time.

The other youth was surprised too, and chagrined

that his trick had failed. But he still wished to marry the old woman's daughter and pleaded with her: "Please give me your real child for my wife."

The old woman hesitated. She thought for a moment and replied: "You are both very dear to me. I must be absolutely fair. Tonight will be a moonless night. I shall put my two daughters each in a separate room. One will be in the east room and the other in the west room. You two will stay outside and when I say 'ready,' you will both come into the house and go to the room of your choice. The girl you find there will be your bride. I'm sure this is the best and fairest plan."

That night the two youths waited outside for the old woman's command.

Suddenly Talltree heard a mosquito flying close to his ear.

"Buss, buzz," said the mosquito, in a wee voice. "Talltree, you must go to the east room. Buzz, buzz. Remember, it is the east room."

Talltree was overjoyed to hear this. He felt sure the mosquito was one he had saved during the flood.

"Ready!" the old woman cried out.

The two boys went into the house. While the other boy was still hestating, Talltree went straight to the east room. There he found the good and beautiful daughter of the old woman. She became his wife.

The other youth could not complain. So he took the other girl for his wife.

Both couples were very, very happy. They had many, many children and lived happily ever after. In time, their children, and their grandchildren, and their great-grandchildren spread throughout the world. And again the earth was filled with people.

15 The Three Little Girls

DEEP in the mountains there stood a lonely hut. In this hut lived a mother and her three small daughters. The eldest girl was named Haisuni, the second Talsuni, and the youngest Peolsuni.

One day the mother had to leave home to take some firewood to a distant market to sell. Before she left she called her three daughters and said: "Listen, Haisuni, Talsuni, and Peolsuni. Do be careful while I am gone, for there is a very bad tiger roaming the woods nearby. Don't ever open the door to anybody until I get back. Otherwise you might be eaten up by the bad tiger."

So saying, the mother stepped out the door and went on her way.

Just as she was leaving, the bad tiger happened to pass the house. He was very hungry and was in search of food. He saw the mother leave the house and thought: "Ho ho! Now's my chance! Now that the mother's gone, I'll be able to eat those three young girls of hers. They should make a tasty dinner for me. How nice that would be!"

The tiger waited a while to make sure that the mother would not return. Then, when he thought the time was ripe, he crept up to the house and called out in his sweetest voice: "Haisuni, Talsuni, Peolsuni —Mother has just come back. Please open the door."

Of course, no matter how sweetly the tiger spoke, his voice was not the voice of their mother. So the eldest girl, Haisuni, asked: "Is that really you, Mother? It doesn't sound a bit like you."

"Why, of course I'm your mother," the tiger answered. "I was invited to a feast and there I sang so many songs that my voice has become hoarse."

The second daughter, Talsuni, then asked: "If you are really our mother, then show us your eyes. We would be able to tell for sure."

Hearing this, the tiger put his blood-shot eyes to a knothole in the front door and peered into the house.

Talsuni saw the red eyes and drew back in surprise. "Oh my! Why are your eyes so red?"

The tiger, a bit confused, hurriedly explained: "I dropped in at Grandfather's house and helped grind some red pepper pods. Some of the pepper got into my eyes, and that's why they are so red."

The third daughter, Peolsuni, next asked: "If that's true, then let us see your hands. We could really tell then whether you are our mother or not."

The tiger put his hairy, yellow paws to a chink in the door.

Peolsuni peeked through the crack and cried: "Why! Your hands are all yellow!"

"Yes, my child," the tiger said, "I was helping our relatives in the next village plaster their house with yellow mud. That's why my hands are so yellow."

In this way the clever tiger fooled all the girls completely. The three sisters, sure that it was their mother, unlocked the front door. And who should come in but a huge, yellow tiger!

"My, you children looked after the house well, didn't you?" the tiger said. "As a reward, Mother will cook a nice dinner for you." The tiger went into the kitchen, his eyes shining with greed.

The three girls stood huddled in a corner, quivering with fear. "What shall we do? What shall we do? We shall soon be eaten up by the tiger."

The three girls quickly ran out of the house. Then tiptoeing softly away, they quickly climbed up a pine tree growing near the well. There they hid quietly in the branches.

The tiger soon noticed that the girls were no longer in the house. "Haisuni, Talsuni, Peolsuni," he called, "where are you?"

And the bad tiger looked here and there, inside and outside the house, everywhere, but nowhere were the girls to be seen. The tiger passed the well and happened to glance in. There he saw in the water the reflection of the three girls hiding in the branches of the pine tree.

"My, children!" the tiger said. "What are you doing up there? I want to come up too, but it looks difficult. Tell Mother how to climb the tree.

At this, Haisuni called down: "There's some sesame oil in the kitchen cupboad. Rub some of the oil on the trunk of the tree. Then you can easily climb up."

Quickly, the tiger went into the house, got the oil, and rubbed it on the trunk of the tree. Then

he tried to climb, but the oil made him slip all the more, and try as he might, he could not reach the girls.

Once again, the tiger looked up into the tree and said: "Be good children, dears, and tell me truly how to climb the tree."

Talsuni, the second daughter, unthinkingly let her tongue slip and said: "There's an ax in the shed. If you cut some notches in the tree trunk, then you can climb up."

Quickly, the tiger went for the ax and began cutting footholds with it. One step at a time, he climbed up and up toward the girls.

The three sisters were desparate. They were sure they would be eaten up. They raised their eyes toward the sky and prayed to the God of Heaven. "Please help us, God. Please send down your golden well bucket," they prayed.

Their prayers were answered, and from the top of a cloud down came a golden well bucket. The three sisters climbed into the bucket and were snatched up, out of the teeth of danger, into the clouds.

When the tiger saw this, he too prayed: "Please send down a well bucket for me also."

Once again, a well bucket came down from the

clouds. But, this time, the rope of the bucket was old and rotten. The tiger, nevertheless, climbed trustingly into the bucket, and it started rising. But when he was half way up to the cloud, the rope suddenly broke, and the tiger came crashing to earth, right in the middle of a millet field.

That is why the root tops of millet are mottled to this day. The reddish spots are from the blood of the tiger which splattered all over the millet field.

On the other hand, the three sisters who climbed to Heaven were each given a special task. Haisuni was made to shine in the sky during the day. Talsuni was made to shine at night. And Peolsuni was to twinkle on nights when Talsuni slept or was on her way from the sky to rest. That is why the sun is called Haisuni, the moon Talsuni, and the stars Peolsuni. To this very day, the three sisters keep at their tasks, taking their turns at brightening the whole world with their light.

16 The Blind Mouse

ONCE there was a very selfish girl. This girl was completely spoiled. Never in her life had she ever said yes to anything. If something displeased her, even in the slightest, she would fuss and fume and fret and make her parents miserable. At the same time, she had to have her own way about everything. She would never listen to others and always wanted her own wishes granted right away.

No matter how often her mother and father told her how bad she was, it did not seem to have any effect. She was always the same spoiled girl.

"What will ever happen to this child of ours?" This was all her parents ever worried about.

One day this little girl was sitting all by herself

in her room, when a small mouse came scampering out of its hole.

"My, how horrible!" she cried in surprise. But, because the mouse was so small and cute, she did not feel afraid. She sat perfectly still and waited to see what would happen.

The little mouse ran here and there around the room in search of something. In one corner of the room a few grains of rice had been spilt. When the mouse found the rice, strangely enough, it did not gobble the rice up, but instead hurried back into its hole.

In a little while, out it came again. This time it was not alone. Out followed a larger mouse. It was the mother mouse.

The little mouse led the mother mouse to the grains of spilt rice. The mother mouse sniffed around with her nose and found the rice grains.

"Squeak, squeak," the mother mouse cried in delight. Then she hungrily gobbled up the rice grains.

You see, the mother mouse was blind. And because she could not see anything, she could not find food for herself without help. So the little mouse always searched out food for the mother mouse.

Presently there was the sound of footsteps outside.

The little mouse cried: "Squeak, squeak, Mother! We must hurry home." Then, it led its mother back into their hole, guarding her all the while with care.

The spoiled girl had been watching this from beginning to end. Now she became thoroughly ashamed of herself. "Why even a little mouse loves and cares for its mother like that. What a bad girl I have been," she told herself.

After that, she changed so completely that everybody thought she was different girl, and all the people praised her for being a good child. She never told anyone about the little mouse and its blind mother.

17 The Deer and the Woodcutter

 LONG, long ago, at the foot of the Kumgang Mountains, there lived a poor woodcutter. He lived alone with his mother, for he had not yet married. Every day he would go into the mountains to cut wood, for that was his job.

One fine autumn day, when the red maple trees flamed everywhere, the woodcutter went as usual to chop wood in the forest. Soon he was hard at his work, for he was an earnest worker. But suddenly a stately deer came running out of the forest. He was panting and seemed almost on the point of falling with exhaustion.

"Save me, please!" the deer cried, "a hunter is chasing me." And he looked back in fear, as if expecting the hunter to come out of the woods at any moment.

The woodcutter felt sorry for the deer and said: "Here, I'll help you. Quick, hide under these branches."

So saying, the woodcutter covered the deer with a small tree he had just felled. No sooner had this been done than a hunter appeared, carrying a gun.

"Say!" the hunter said. "Didn't a deer come running this way?"

"Yes," the woodcutter answered with a straight face, "but he kept on going that way."

The hunter quickly ran in the direction the woodcutter had pointed.

After the hunter was gone, the deer, who had kept still as death till now, came out. "Thank you very much," he said. "You saved me from great danger. I shall never forget you kindness." The deer thanked the woodcutter many, many times and then disappeared into the forest.

Some days later the deer came again to where the woodcutter was working and said: "I have come today to repay you for saving my life. Do you not wish to have a beautiful wife?"

The woodcutter blushed. "Of course, I want a

bride. But who would want to marry such a poor
man as I?"

"Don't say that. Just listen to me. If you do as I say,
you will be able to get a good wife this very day. All
you have to do is..." Then the deer put his mouth
to the woodcutter's ears and began whispering:
"If you cross that divide and go straight on, you
will come to a large pond. Often beautiful fairies
come down from Heaven to bathe in that pool. They
are sure to be there today. If you start out now, you
will be able to see them. When you get there, take
just one of the robes which the fairies have hung on
the trees while they bathe, and hide it carefully.
Remember, take only one. Their robes are made of
very fine feathers, and without them the fairies cannot fly back to Heaven. Thus there will be one fairy
who will be left without her robe. Take that fairy
home, and she will become your bride. Do you
understand? Remember, take only one robe. You
will surely succeed, so leave right away."

The woodcutter listened carefully, but it seemed
like a dream story, and he looked as if he could not
believe the deer's story.

But the deer said: "Don't worry. Do just as
you are told."

At this, the woodcutter decided to give it a try. "Then I shall go and see," he said.

As he started out, the deer called him back and said: "Oh, there is one more thing. After the fairy has become your bride, you must be very careful until she has borne you four children. No matter how she may ask, you must never bring out her robe of feathers nor show it to her. If you do, there will be great trouble."

The woodcutter climbed straight up the path the deer had shown him. He crossed the mountain divide and, sure enough, presently he came to a large pond. And in the pond, he saw a number of fairies bathing, as beautiful as those painted in pictures. Hanging on the trees were many, many shining robes of feathers, as light and thin as gossamer.

"So these are the robes of feathers the deer spoke about," thought the woodcutter. Quietly, he took one from a tree and folded it over and over. So fine was the robe that it folded thin into the thickness of a single sheet of paper. The woodcutter then carefully hid the robe in his breast pocket. Then he sat down in the shade of a nearby tree and watched the fairies from a distance.

Soon the fairies finished their bathing and came

up from the pond to put on their robes. Everyone had a robe to wear, all except one fairy. Her robe was missing. She looked all over, but it was not to be found. The other fairies were worried, and they too joined in the search. They looked high and low, but the robe was nowhere.

After a long while, the sun began to set, and the fairies said: "We can't keep looking forever. If it becomes too late, the gates of Heaven will be closed. We will have to leave you here alone, but when we get back to Heaven we shall talk with the others and try to do something to help you." Then they spread out the hems of their robes and flew up into the sky, leaving the one poor fairy all by herself beside the pond.

Thus the fairy who had no feathered robe was finally taken home by the poor woodcutter and became his bride.

The two were very happy, and the woodcutter counted himself very fortunate. Once the fairy had become the woodcutter's wife, she seemed to forget all about returning to Heaven, and she worked earnestly in her new home. She cared faithfully for her mother-in-law and for her husband. Then one, two, three children were born to them, and she raised the children with loving care.

The woodcutter soon lost all fear that

his wife might one day leave him. His wife never once mentioned the robe of feathers, and the wood-cutter never mentioned it himself. But he still remembered the words of the deer, telling him that he must never show his wife the robe until four children were born.

One evening after a hard day's work, the wood-cutter was seated at home, drinking the wine his wife was serving him with loving care.

"I never knew that the world of man was such a pleasant place to live in," his wife remarked casually. "I wouldn't even dream of returning to Heaven. But isn't it strange? I often wonder where my robe of feathers disappeared to. Could it be possible that you hid it?"

The woodcutter was an honest man at heart. So when his wife asked him thus about the robe, some-how he couldn't bring himself to pretend ignorance. Besides, his wife had now borne him three children, and he could not lie to her. The rice wine, too, had gone slightly to his head, and he was caught off guard.

"I have kept it a secret until now," he said, "but you're right—it was I who hid your robe."

"Oh," she answered with a smile, "so it *was* you,

after all. I often thought it might be so. When I think of the past, I feel a pang of yearning for old things. I wonder how the robe looks after all these years. Please let me take a look at it for a moment."

Somehow, the woodcutter felt relieved at having told his wife the secret he had kept hidden all to himself these many years. Forgetting all about the deer's warning, he gladly brought out the robe and showed it to her.

His wife spread the beautiful robe in her hands, and, as she did so, there stirred in her heart a strange and indescribable feeling. A snatch of an old song rose to her lips:

> *The multi-colored clouds now spread,*
> *Gold and silver, purple and red;*
> *And the strains of a heavenly sound*
> *In the balmy skies redound....*

From the robe of feathers held in her hands, memories of dreamy days lived in Heaven now returned with startling clarity, and she was filled with an uncontrollable homesickness.

Suddenly she placed the robe lightly on her shoulders. Then she put one child on her back and the other two under each arm.

"Farewell, my husband," she said, "I must, after

all, go back to Heaven." And with these words she rose into the air.

The woodcuter was so astounded that he could not move for a while. When he was finally able to run outside, there his wife was, high in the sky, looking like a tiny dragonfly winging its way to Heaven.

No matter how much the woodcutter sighed in regret over his mistake, it was now too late. He no longer had the will to go to work. Every day he stayed at home, staring into the sky and sighing for his wife and children.

One day the deer that he had saved came visiting. The deer already knew that the woodcutter's wife had returned to Heaven, taking with her the three children.

"Didn't I tell you so?" the deer said. "If there had been four children, this would never have happened. You see, a mother cannot leave a child behind. If you had had four children, she could not have carried the fourth and so couldn't have left you."

Spoken to like this by the deer, the woodcutter felt even more ashamed of himself. All he could do was hang his head and continue sighing.

"But," the deer continued, "don't be too disheart-

ened. There is still a way you can be reunited with
her. You remember that pond, don't you? Since the
day the robe was lost, the fairies no longer come down
to earth. Instead, they send down a bucket on a rope
from Heaven and draw up water from that pond.
Apparently the water of that pond is better even than
the water in Heaven.

"Now, this is what you should do. Go to the pond
and wait. When the bucket is lowered and filled
with water, hurry and empty it out. Then climb inside the bucket yourself, and you will be drawn up
into Heaven."

Again the woodcutter did as the deer told him.
And he really did get to Heaven. There he was able
to meet his dear wife and children again. His wife
was once again a fairy, but she was overjoyed to see
her husband and greeted him with open arms.

Many, many happy days followed for them. The
woodcutter's life in Heaven was like a dream.
Heaven was beautiful beyond belief. Never had the
woodcutter seen or even imagined such beautiful
scenery. His every day was an ecstasy of delight.

But there was one thing that troubled him. He
often thought of his mother, whom he had left behind
in the village at the foot of the Kumgang Mountains.

Time and time again, he asked himself: "I wonder
what Mother is doing now? She surely must be
lonely, living all by herself." And every time he
thought of his mother, he kept saying: "If I could
only see her just once, I would be very, very happy."

His wife, the fairy, said: "If you are so worried
about her, why don't you go to see her? I'll bring
you a heavenly horse, which will take you to Mother's
place in a moment." So she brought him a heavenly
horse.

As her husband was mounting the horse, the fairy
said: "Listen! There is one important thing to remember. You must never get off this horse. If
you so much as set a single foot on the ground, you
will never be able to return to Heaven. Whatever
happens, don't ever dismount. Do everything that
you must do sitting on the horse." Only after the
fairy had repeated this instruction over and over
again did she finally allow her husband to set out
on his journey.

As soon as the woodcutter was firmly mounted, the
heavenly horse whinnied once and was off like a
bolt of lightning. In no time at all they reached
the village at the foot of the Kumgang Mountains.

The aged mother had been living a lonely life

all alone. When she saw her son atop a horse at her door, she wept with joy.

But the woodcutter would not get off his horse. "Mother," he said, "I am so glad to see you well. Please take good care of yourself and stay strong and well forever. If I get off this horse, I cannot go back to Heaven, and so I must say farewell as I am." So saying, the woodcutter pulled on his reins and was about to set off for Heaven.

The mother was loath to part with her son. "You have come such a long way," she said. "How can you leave like this? If you cannot dismount, then at least have a bowl of your favorite pumpkin soup. I remember how you used to love it so. I have just made some, and it should be just about ready now."

The mother went inside the house and soon returned with a steaming bowl of hot soup for her son.

The woodcutter could not refuse his mother's kindness and took the soupbowl from her hand, still seated on the horse. But, what should happen? The bowl was so hot that the woodcutter dropped it as soon as it touched his hands.

The soup splashed all over the horse's back. The horse jumped with a start and reared back on its hind legs. The woodcutter was thrown to the ground.

With a great neigh of pain, the horse leaped into the sky, leaving the woodcutter behind. In a twinkling of an eye, the horse was gone from sight.

Once again the woodcutter was left on earth. But this time, no matter how he grieved and cried, it was no use. Day after day the woodcutter lifted his face to the sky and called again and again to his wife and his children. But it was too late. Even his friend, the deer, could no longer help him. Day and night the woodcutter yearned to return to Heaven. Day and night he yearned to see his wife and children again. And as he kept gazing up into the sky and calling to his loved ones year after year, he was finally transformed into a rooster.

That is why, when country children today see a rooster atop a straw-thatched roof crowing out the time, they remember this story, told them by their grandparents, of the woodcutter crying for his wife and children.

18   The Magic Gem

 ONCE upon a time there was an old fisherman. He lived with his wife in a small hut on the bank of a large river.

One day, as usual, he went to the river to fish. All day long he cast his line, but he did not catch a single fish, not even a minnow. He thought of returning home empty-handed, but he could not give up and once again threw his line into the water.

This time there was a big tug and, when he pulled out his line, he found that he had caught a huge carp. The old man was overjoyed. But, as he put the carp into his creel, he noticed that the fish's eyes were full of tears. On top of that, the carp was opening and shutting its mouth, as if it were trying to say something. The fisherman was suddenly struck with pity for the poor fish.

"Oh, you're trying to say let me go, are you not?" he said. "Yes, I understand. So I'll let you go."

So saying, the gentle old man put the fish back in the river and set it free. He then slung his empty wicker creel on his shoulder and started home. He knew that he and his wife would have nothing for supper. Yet, somehow, he felt clean and good for having freed the carp.

The next morning the fisherman was back at the river fishing. Suddenly a beautiful youth, wearing a crown on his head, stood before him, bowing politely.

The old man was taken aback and asked: "Who are you?"

The youth bowed again, deeply, and replied: "I am a messenger from the Palace of the Dragon King. The carp you saved yesterday is really the prince of the Dragon Palace. Thanks to your mercy, he returned safely home. The king of the Dragon Palace was deeply moved when he heard how you saved his son's life, and he wishes to repay you. He invites you to visit him and sent me to bring you back. Please come with me immediately."

No sooner had the youth said this than he mumbled

some strange words as though chanting a magic spell. Suddenly the waters of the river parted in two, and before the fisherman's eyes there appeared a beautiful road, the like of which he had never seen before.

The old fisherman could not tell whether he was dreaming or not. But he did as the youth bade him, rising to his feet and following the young man.

The two walked on and on, straight down the beautiful road. It seemed it would never come to an end, when suddenly there appeared before them the Dragon Palace. It was a sight to surprise anyone, for it was indeed a beautiful place. The old fisherman had often heard stories of the Dragon Palace, but never in his wildest dreams had he imagined it to be so beautiful.

The Dragon King was waiting outside the palace and greeted the old fisher-man with open arms. The prince also came out to welcome the old man, and to thank him.

"I am the carp you caught yesterday. I have you to thank for saving my life, yet I do not know how to express my gratitude to you," the prince said.

The old fisherman felt as if he were in a trance. The king spread a great feast before him, and a host of fish came out to entertain him. There was a bream, and then a sole, who performed special dances for the honored guest.

Day after day was spent thus in feasting and merry-making. But, amid these pleasures, the old fisherman began worrying about his wife and home. His worries mounted with the passing of days. He thought how lonely his wife must be all by herself.

The prince noticed how restless the old man had become and said: "You need not worry any longer. You may return home any time you want. But there is one thing I would like to tell you before you leave. My father will be sure to give you a present on your departure. When he offers you somthing, you must say you do not want anything but the green gem that is kept in the palace treasure box. As long as you have this magic gem, you can wish for anything you desire, and your wish will be granted. Don't forget. Be sure to ask for the green gem."

As the old man prepared to leave, the king called him and said: "I hear you are going home, my good man, and want to give you a present. What would you like as a remembrance of your stay here?"

The old man remembered what the prince had told him and answered: "The only thing I want is the green gem in your treasure box."

A troubled look came over the king's face. "I cannot give you that," he said, "but I will give you anything else."

The prince then spoke up: "Father, true the green gem is a very precious thing, but remember this man saved my life. I am sure the gem is small reward enough when you think that I am well and sound today thanks to this old fisherman."

When he heard this, the king reluctantly brought out the green gem from his treasure box and handed it to the old fisherman. The old man thanked the two and bade them farewell. The youth with the crown on his head then led the old man back along the road through the river to the river bank. And the fisherman was soon safe at his own home.

During the fisherman's absence, his wife had worried constantly. She could not imagine what had happened to him. So she was overjoyed when he returned safely. The old man told his wife how he had been taken to the Dragon Palace for saving the life of a carp and how he had been given a green gem as a farewell present. He brought out the gem and explained that, through its power, their every wish would be fulfilled.

The old woman said: "If that's true, let's test it. I wish we had a large and beautiful home."

No sooner had she said this than their old straw-thatched hut disappeared, and in its place there stood a splendid mansion.

The old man and old woman were very pleased, and they wished next for rice and wheat and red beans. The magic gem produced as much of these as the old couple desired.

There was now enough for the two to eat for many days. The green gem also brought them much silver and gold. It brought them, in fact, whatever they desired. The old man and woman, who had lived in poverty all their lives, were now able to enjoy the life of the rich, wanting for nothing.

Across the river there happened to live a bad old woman. When this woman heard of the good fortune that had come to the old fisherman and his wife, she was filled with envy. "I must get that green gem somehow or other," she mumbled to herself. And she schemed and schemed as to how she could get it.

One day she hit upon a good plan. She waited until the old man was away from home and then dressed herself up to look like a cloth-peddler. Then she called on the fisherman's wife.

"My, what a beautiful home you have!" she said in her most flattering voice. "I have heard that you have a magic gem given you by the King of the Dragon Palace. I'd just love to see what it looks like. Could you not let me see it, just for a minute? I'd *so* like to tell my friends that I've seen the green gem from the Dragon Palace."

The honest fisherman's wife was completely taken in by the polite manner and flattering tone of the cloth-peddler. "Why, of course," she said. "That's a simple request. I'll gladly bring it out to show you. You may look at it as much as you like."

The good-hearted woman went into her home and brought out the green gem. She handed it over to the false cloth-peddler. The bad woman took the gem and ogled it greedily.

"It's so good of you to let me see it," she said. "It is beautiful indeed." The bad woman turned the gem this way and that and gazed at it from all sides. Then, while the fisherman's wife was not looking, she slipped the gem into her pocket and brought out a green stone that looked exactly like the green gem. But it was only an ordinary stone, without any of the magic powers of the green gem.

"Thank you very much for showing me your treasure," the bad woman said. "You must take good care of it." Then she handed the false gem to the fisherman's wife and quickly took her departure.

No sooner had the bad woman gone than the beautiful, tiled mansion completely disappeared, and, as the fisherman's wife watched with horror, in its stead there appeared the old straw-thatched hut in which she and her husband had first lived.

"What has happened?" cried the fisherman's wife. "How could this be?" Then she suddenly realized that the cloth-peddler must have tricked her. She ran outside, but the cloth-peddler was nowhere in sight.

"What shall I do? What shall I do?" moaned the fisherman's wife. "How will I be able to explain all this to my husband?" She looked at the miserable shack and shed bitter, bitter tears, but there was nothing she could do to recover the magic gem.

The fisherman returned after a while and was astounded to find his fine house gone. "What happened to our home?" he asked his wife.

But the old woman was too grief-stricken to say a word. All she did was sob and weep.

The beautiful mansion, the riches, and the happiness of the old couple were now things of the past. They had faded away like yesterday's dream. The old man and woman sat huddled in their miserable hut, not speaking a word to each other, each wondering what they should do on the morrow.

Now, the old man and the old woman had a pet dog and a pet cat. Since they had no offspring, they loved this dog and cat as if they were their own children. Seeing the old fisherman and wife wailing over the loss of the green gem, the dog and the cat got together to discuss what they could do to help.

"Let's get back the green gem for the old man and old woman," said the dog.

"Yes, they have both been good to us all these years. Now is the time we should try and repay them," the cat chimed in.

The dog and the cat knew that the cloth-peddler

was really the bad woman from across the river in disguise. So they immediately set out for the bad woman's house. When they came to the river, the cat got on the dog's back, and the dog jumped into the river and swam to the other shore. They climbed up the bank and saw a large and beautiful house that they had never seen before.

"That must be the house of the bad woman who stole the green gem. The gem be hidden somewhere inside the house," the dog said.

The dog and the cat crept up to the house and slipped into the yard to take a good look around. Not knowing she was being spied on, the bad old woman happened to look out from one of the rooms.

"Yes, there she is! That's the bad woman," the cat said, "that's the cloth-peddler who came to our home."

Then the cat jumped lightly up onto the porch and quickly slipped into house. There were so many rooms that she could not tell where the green gem was hidden. But the clever cat kept peeking into one room after another.

"The green gem is a great treasure. The bad woman wouldn't leave it just any place. It must be hidden in the innermost room," the cat thought. So she made her way to the room at the very back of the house. There she spied a cupboard.

"Aha! That would be the most likely place for her to hide the green gem," the cat thought and quietly tried to open the cupboard door.

The bad woman must have heard the cat for she came running frantically into the room. "Scat, you cat!" she cried. "What are you doing here?"

What a frightful face she had! She snatched up the cat and threw her out of the house.

"Now I know where the green gem is hidden," thought the cat and went back to where the dog was waiting for her in the yard.

"How was it?" the dog asked impatiently. "Did you find out where it is hidden."

"Yes, I did," answered the cat, "but the problem now is how to get it back. It's kept in the cupboard in the innermost room."

"Oh, don't worry," the dog replied, "as long as we know where it is, we shall find some way to get it back. But say, aren't you hungry? I'm famished." Come to think of it, neither the dog nor the cat had eaten any supper.

"I'll go look for some food," the cat said. "You just wait here a little while longer." So once again, the cat set off alone, this time to find food, leaving the dog to keep watch in the yard.

"Where can I find something good to eat?" the cat thought, as she prowled through the house.

Suddenly, she heard a commotion coming from inside the storeroom. The cat softly tiptoed to the storeroom and peeked inside. There fifty or sixty mice were gathered together having a grand feast.

The cat watched the proceedings for a while. Then she suddenly leaped into the room and pounced on the king of the mice, who was seated in the place of honor. The cat grabbed the mouse by its neck with her paws and pinned it to the floor. The other mice scampered about the room, screeching and squeaking in great confusion.

The cat called out to the mice to be quiet: "Listen you mice! In the innermost room of this house there is a cupboard. Inside the cupboard there is green gem

hidden away. Bring me that gem immediately. If you do not, I shall eat your king right on the spot!" The cat purposely made fierce eyes and glared at the mice.

The mice were all upset, but they quickly answered: "Please wait awhile. We shall get the green gem for you for sure. Such a task is no trouble at all. We shall bring it right back to you. Please spare our king."

Then five or six of the mice, the ones with the strongest teeth, scampered out of the storeroom. And, sure enough, before long they were back again with the green gem.

As soon as the mice handed the gem over to the cat, she let the king mouse go and, thanking the mice, returned to the yard where the dog was standing watch. The dog too was overjoyed.

"Now that we have the gem, we have nothing

more to do here. Let's get home as fast as we can and make the old man and old woman happy," they said.

Then, completely forgetting their hunger in their hurry to get home, the two set off on their return trip.

The dog and the cat came once again to the river. The cat put the precious green gem in her mouth and jumped on the dog's back. The dog entered the water and began swimming across the river.

When they came to a point midway between the banks of the river, the dog suddenly began worrying about the green gem.

"Is the green gem safe?" the dog asked, continuing to swim.

The cat, of course, could not answer, no matter how much she wanted to, because she had the gem in her mouth. So she remained silent.

The dog asked again: "Are you sure the gem is safe?" Again the cat was silent.

The dog became really worried and asked the same question four or five times. But each time, the cat gave no reply. Finally, the dog lost his patience and became angry.

"Why don't you answer me?" he shouted rudely "Can't you hear me? I've asked you over and over again, and you haven't said a single word in reply."

This made the cat angry too. She could keep quiet no longer. She opened her mouth and cried: "Yes! I have it!"

But as she spoke, the green gem fell out of her mouth and dropped into the river. "Plunk!" fell the gem, deep into the water.

When the dog heard this noise, he suddenly realized what had happened. He felt terribly ashamed of his own stupidity. The cat was furious, but the dog was so ashamed of himself he couldn't find words to apologize. And as soon as he reached the other side of the river, he quietly slunk away home by himself.

On the other hand, the cat could not get over her disappointment. They had gone to all that trouble to get back the green gem, and now it lay at the bottom of the river. The cat sat down by the river, filled with regret and desolation, and pondered on what she should do next.

How long she sat there, she did not know. But, before she realized it, dawn had already broken, and a fisherman came along in his boat to haul in the nets which he had left out all night in the river.

The fisherman began taking fish from the net and

throwing them into his boat. Presently he came upon a dead fish caught in his net. "This fish is no good. I'll throw it away," he said and threw the dead fish up on the river bank as far as he could.

The dead fish landed just beside the cat. The hungry cat picked it up and was starting to eat it when she noticed a hard bulge in the fish's throat. She opened the fish up to see what it was and to her amazement found that it was the green gem which had fallen into the river.

"The fish must have thought the gem was something to eat," reasoned the cat, "and must have swallowed it in one gulp. But the gem was so big that it stuck in the fish's throat. Then the fish must have choked to death. That's why it was dead when found in the net."

Whatever the case, the cat jumped for sheer joy. This time she was not going to lose the gem. She put it carefully in her mouth and hurried straight home. The old man and the old woman could hardly believe their eyes when they saw the green gem.

Once again, the gem gave them a fine home. It gave them rice and wheat. It gave them silver and gold.

The old man and the old woman praised the cat for bringing back the green gem. Out of gratitude, they allowed the cat to come inside the house and to live there from that time forth, eating the best of foods. But the dog, for his stupidity, was forced to sleep in a corner of the yard and given nothing but left-over food and fish bones to eat.

Because the cat became such a favorite the dog was very jealous of her. From that day on the cat and the dog became enemies. And that is why, even today, cats and dogs always fight on sight.

19 The Snake and the Toad

ONCE there lived a very kind and gentle maiden in a remote country village. She was very poor and barely managed to eke out a living for herself and her aged mother, whom she had to care for all alone. One day the girl was in the kitchen, just scooping up freshly-cooked rice and putting it into a large bowl to carry to the dinner table. Suddenly a toad appeared in the kitchen as if from nowhere. It crawled over the floor laboriously, dragging its body, right up to where the girl was standing. Then it jumped heavily up onto the kitchen hearth. On the hearth were a few grains of rice which the girl had spilled while emptying the pot. The toad ate up the rice hungrily.

"My, you must really be hungry," the kind-hearted girl said. "Here, I'll give you some more."

And she spilled about half a ladleful of rice out on the hearth. The toad looked up at the girl in gratitude and then gobbled up that rice too, all the while wriggling his puffy throat.

From that day on the girl and the toad became fast friends. The toad did not go anywhere. He made his home in a corner of the kitchen and would come out at mealtimes to eat his share of rice right out of the girl's hands. This way of life continued day after day, until one whole year had passed. By this time the toad had grown into a huge creature.

Now, this village had been troubled for a long, long time by a huge snake that lived in a nest on the outskirts of the hamlet. It was a bad snake. It played havoc with the rice paddies and the vegetable fields. It stole cows and horses. It even kidnapped women and children and dragged them away to its nest, where it ate them up at leisure. This had happened not once or twice, but many, many times.

The villagers knew the hide-out of the snake. Its nest was in a huge cave in a rocky hill just outside the village. Master bowmen and famed marksmen came in turn to the great snake's nest to try and kill the monster, but none succeeded. Year after year the snake continued to harass the villagers. The people lived constantly under the threat of death. They never knew when the snake would come forth from its nest and pounce upon the unsuspecting. They never knew where it would strike next. The villagers lived in constant fear.

The toad's friend, the kind-hearted girl, soon came to the point where she could not bear to see the sufferings of the village people. Without really knowing when, she found herself thinking: "The villagers must be saved. There must be some way. Isn't there a good scheme?"

But when bows and arrows and guns had failed to kill the snake, what could one lone and weak girl do? After much pondering, the girl finally decided that she would give up her own life to save the villagers from this curse.

"That's it!" she thought. "If a large number of people can be saved, it doesn't matter what happens to me. I shall offer myself to be eaten by the great snake, and I shall entreat the snake never again to terrorize our village. Where guns and arrows have failed, my sincere pleas might succeed."

Her old mother was now dead, and she was all

alone in the world except for her friend the toad. So, once she had made her mind up, she put on her little shoes with their turned-up toes and slipped out of the house. Just before leaving she called the toad and, wiping the tears from her eyes, said: "We have lived happily together for a long time, haven't we? But today is our last day. I must say goodbye. There will be no one to give you your rice tomorrow. When you become hungry, you will have to go out and find your own food."

The toad, of course, had no way of understanding the language of human beings. But the girl spoke to it in simple and gentle words, just as if she were talking to a child. All the while the toad squatted on the hearth gazing steadily up at the girl's face.

The girl finally wound her way to the snake's nest in the rocky hill outside the village. Forgetting her fear and her sorrow in her desire to save the villagers, she stepped right up to the mouth of the snake's nest. "I have come in place of the villagers to offer you my life," she said. "Please eat me. But, after this, please never again bother the village people."

Nothing happened, so the girl continued speaking thus for a long time. Soon night drew near,

and darkness began to fall over the countryside.

Finally, when the last light of day faded, the earth began to tremble, and the snake came out of its hole. Its scales were a gleaming green, its red tongue was like a flame. When the girl saw the terrible appearance of the snake, she fainted on the spot and fell to the ground.

Just then a single streak of white poison flashed toward the snake. It came from the toad which the girl had cared for with such kindness. No one

knew when it had come, but there it was, squatting right beside the girl. And though it was small compared to the snake, it was squirting poison with all its might to protect the unconscious girl.

But the snake was not to be beaten so easily. It began spewing poison right back at the toad. Thus the snake and the toad matched poison against poison, the jets of poison crossing and criss-crossing in the air like two sharp darts. Neither would give in. This continued for one hour, two hours. There was no sound of clashing swords, no shouts of battle. For all that, it was a deadly fight, waged in grim silence.

Gradually, the snake's poison began to weaken. On the other hand, the toad's poison became stronger and stronger. And yet, the fight still continued.

Suddenly the snake let out a great gasp and fell down on the rocky hillside. Its great body twitched once, twice, and then it was dead. At the same time the toad, worn out with its struggle, fell dead too. The battle was finally at an end.

A lone villager chanced by the scene of the fighting the next morning and found the small girl still unconscious. He took her to her home and nursed her back to health. In this way, not only was the girl saved but the whole village as well—thanks to the heroic struggle of a lone toad whom the maiden had befriended. Now that the evil snake was dead, the villagers were able to live in peace and quiet.

20 The Pheasant's Bell

DEEP in a lonely forest there once lived a woodcutter. One day the woodcutter was at work felling trees, when he heard the cry of a pheasant and the fluttering of wings nearby. He wondered what was happening and went to see what the commotion was about. Under the shade of a bush he saw a pheasant nest with many eggs inside it. A great snake was poised to strike at a mother pheasant, who was bravely trying to defend her nest. The woodcutter picked up a stick and tried to scare the snake away, crying: "Go away! Go away!" But the snake wouldn't move, so the woodcutter struck it with his stick and killed it.

Some years after this, the woodcutter one day set

out on a distant journey. Twilight found him walking along a lonely mountain path. Soon it became
completely dark. He was hungry and tired. Suddenly, far ahead of him in the woods he saw a dim
light. He walked toward this light and came to
a large and beautiful straw-thatched house. The
woodcutter was surprised, for he had never expected
to find such a fine house so deep in the forest. He
knocked on the door, and a beautiful girl, about
nineteen or twenty years of age, came out.

"I am hungry and tired," the woodcutter told her.
"I have walked a long way today and have no place
to stay. I wonder if you would put me up for the
night?"

The girl answered in a kind tone: "I am alone in
this house, but please do come in."

She welcomed the woodcutter inside and spread

out a grand feast for him. But
the woodcutter felt very ill at
ease. He could not understand
why such a beautiful young
girl should be living all alone
in the middle of a forest. He
couldn't help wondering if he
hadn't entered a haunted house.

But he was so hungry that he ate the fine food put before him and asked no questions. Only when he was quite full did he finally speak.

"Why should such a young person as you live all alone here in such a large house?" he asked.

"I am waiting to take my revenge against my enemy," the girl answered.

"Your enemy?" he asked. "Where would he be?"

"He is right here," she said. "See, you are my enemy!" Then she opened a great red mouth and laughed loudly.

The woodcutter was astounded and asked her why he should be her enemy.

The girl reminded him of the time he had saved the mother pheasant and her nest, and added: "I am the snake you killed that time. I've waited a long long time to meet up with you. And now I'm going to take your life. Then finally I'll have the revenge I've dreamed of so long."

When the woodcutter heard this, his heart sank. "I had nothing against you at that time," he said in a quavering voice. "It was simply because I couldn't bear to see helpless beings hurt by someone strong like you were. That's why I saved the pheasant. But I really didn't mean to kill you. Don't say I'm your enemy. Please, please spare my life."

At first the girl kept laughing at him and would not listen to has pleas. But he kept on pleading, from bended knees, with tears flowing down his cheeks.

"All right then," the girl said, "I'll give you one chance. Deep in the forest and high in the mountains there is a temple ruin. Not a single soul lives there. However, a huge bell hangs in that temple. If, before dawn, you are able to ring that bell without moving from the place where you're sitting now, then I'll spare your life."

When the woodcutter heard this, he was even more frightened. "How can I ring that bell while I'm still sitting here in this room?" he sighed. "You're unfair. I'm no better off than before. Please don't say such a cruel thing. It's the same as killing me right now. Please let me go home."

The girl firmly refused: "No! You are the enemy I've waited for so long. Yes, I've waited a long time for this chance to avenge myself. Now that I have you in my hands, why should I let you go? If you can't ring the bell, resign yourself to death. I shall eat you up."

The woodcutter gave up all hope. He realized

that he was as good as dead.

Suddenly, the quiet night air vibrated with the sound of a distant bell. "Bong!" the bell rang. Yes, it was the bell in the crumbling old mountain temple!

When the girl heard the bell, she turned white and gnashed her teeth. "It's no use," she said. "You must be guarded by the gods."

No sooner had she said this than she disappeared from sight. The fine house in which the woodcutter was sitting also disappeared in a puff of smoke.

The woodcutter, whose life had been so miraculously saved, could hardly wait for daylight to break. With the first sign of dawn he set off toward the mountains in search of the ruined temple, filled with gnawing curiosity.

Sure enough, as he had been told, there he found a temple in which hung a great bell. But there was not a single soul in sight. The woodcutter looked at the bell in wonder. On it he noticed a stain of blood. He looked down to the floor. There, with head shattered and wings broken, lay the blood-stained body of a pheasant.

21 The Green Leaf

DAY in, day out, the rain poured down in sheets. The small river flowing by the village rose higher and higher. One day the dikes broke. The muddy river water surged through the gap, sweeping everything in its path—houses, people, cows, and horses. Everywhere was death and devastation.

Just then there appeared in the raging waters an old man, rowing a small boat. He was a gentle and kind man. He could not bear to remain in safety while listening to the cries of people stranded on tree-tops and on roof-tops. He rowed his small boat here and there, helping as many people as he could to places of safety.

Just as he was about to leave he saw a small child

struggling in the water. He pulled the child into his boat. He next saw a deer swimming by. The deer too he saved. A little while later a snake came swimming by. The old man looked carefully and saw that it had hurt itself. It couldn't swim very well. A snake is not a very pleasant thing, but the old man felt sorry for it. He reached into the swirling waters and pulled the snake into the boat.

When he reached high ground, the old man let the snake and the deer go free. But the child had nowhere to go. He had lost his home, his parents, and his brothers and sisters. He was now an orphan. The old man felt pity for the poor little boy. He seemed such a clever fellow, with fine features. Since the old man was childless, he decided to adopt the boy as his own. "You will become my boy from this day," the old man said, and from then on he cared for him as if he were his own child.

One day much later the old man was puttering about the house. Suddenly the same deer that he had saved during the flood came to the house. The deer came right up to the old man inside the house, nudged him with its nose as though glad to see him, and made happy sounds in its throat. Then the deer took hold of the old man's sleeve in its mouth and started pulling. The deer kept pulling at the old man as though wanting him to follow it.

"You want me to go outside with you, do you?" the old man said. "Yes, that must be it."

So the old man went outside with the deer. The deer kept going on ahead, and the old man followed. The deer went on and on, toward the mountains. Up and up they climbed. The old man didn't know where they were going. Neither could he imagine what the deer wanted.

Just as they crossed a mountain divide, the deer stopped short and waited for the old man to catch up. There in the mountain was a cave. The deer led the old man to the mouth of the cave and then went in ahead. The old man followed. And in the middle of the cave he found a large box filled to overflowing with gold and silver, shining with such dazzling brightness as to blind the eyes. The old man took this treasure home.

Thanks to the deer, the old man was now very wealthy. He bought a large mansion and many fields and paddies. He came to live a life of plenty. And his adopted son quickly learned to live an easy-going life. He learned to be selfish and extravagant.

He spent money like water, he made friends with good-for-nothing youths, and he frittered his days away in idleness.

The old man began to worry over the future of his son. He tried to advise the youngster, but his words fell on deaf ears. Eventually the young man came to talk back to his foster father. He went from bad to worse and, in time, even started spreading a base lie about his father.

"That old man didn't get his money from the deer. That's a black lie. He stole all of it during the flood from people who were washed away." This was the lie the youngster spread all over the village.

When this lie came to the ears of the overlord, the

old man was hauled off to the overlord's castle for questioning.

"That's simply not true," the old man insisted. "The deer really did lead me to the money in a cave."

But no mater how earnestly and how often the old man repeated this to the castle officials, they still doubted him.

"Even your adopted son, whom you brought up yourself for so many years, says you stole your wealth," they said. "Isn't that sufficient proof of your crime?" And they threw him into the castle dungeon.

There was nothing the old man could do about it. He spent long hours and days in the dungeon,

crying and waiting for the day he would be brought out to hear his sentence.

But one day while the old man sat despondently in the dungeon, something came moving across the floor. It was the snake the old man had saved during the flood. The snake slithered across the cell to where the old man was sitting and suddenly bit him sharply on the shin. Then it quickly slipped out again.

The old man was greatly grieved. "How unfortunate I am! No matter how lowly a creature may be, to think that it would do such a terrible thing after I went to the trouble of saving its life! I should never have shown pity for that snake." First it was his adopted son and now it was the snake. The old man had saved both from the raging waters, and they had turned against him in ingratitude. The thought filled the old man's breast with such anguish that he felt his heart would burst. He pressed the snake bite with his hands and let the tears stream unashamedly down his cheeks.

Suddenly the snake once again came into his cell. This time it was carrying something in its mouth. It was a green leaf. The snake applied the green leaf to the spot where it had bitten the old man and then quickly disappeared again.

Then a strange thing happened. No sooner had the green leaf been placed on the wound than the pain disappeared, and the swelling also went down almost immediately.

"What was the snake trying to do?" pondered the old man. "First it comes and bites me and then it brings a green leaf that heals me. Why?"

But before he could think further, there was a great commotion outside his cell. "It's terrible, terrible!" the jailers were shouting. "What shall we do? The Lord's consort has just been bitten by a snake. There's no time to call a doctor."

The old man suddenly realized the meaning of the snake's behavior. He shouted: "Let me cure her! I have a wonderful medicine for snake bites!"

The jailers looked doubtfully at the old man.

But it was no time to stop and argue. They let the old man out of his cell and rushed him off to where the overlord's wife lay moaning and suffering in pain. All the old man did was to press the green leaf lightly against the snake bite, and the great lady was completely healed.

The overlord was very pleased and had the old man brought before him. "Old man, where did you get that wonderful medicine?" the lord asked.

The old man then told the overlord all that had befallen him from the time he saved his adopted son, the deer, and the snake in the great flood, until the time the snake appeared in his cell.

"Even such a lowly creature as the snake knows enough to repay a debt of gratitude. But what a hateful man it is who would betray the foster father who saved his life!" the lord said in great anger. Then the lord ordered his men to bring the boy to the castle and to throw him into the dungeon.

The kind and gentle old man was praised highly and heaped with many, many gifts. But, as a last request, he asked that his ungrateful son be released from prison. The overlord was deeply impressed by the compassion of the old man and immediately granted his request. Then the old man and his son made their way home together.

The youth had learned his lesson well. Not only once, but twice, had his life been saved by his foster father. From then on, he became a changed person and grew into an upright and righteous man. He took good care of his father, and they were able to live a long and happy life together.

22 The Grateful Tiger

ONCE upon a time a huge tiger lay groaning and moaning by the roadside. A young student happened to pass by and see the suffering animal. He drew near, half in fear, and asked: "What is the matter, tiger? Have you hurt yourself?"

The tiger, tears filling his eyes, opened its mouth as if to show the student that there was something wrong inside.

"Let me see," the student said, "maybe I can help." The student peered into the tiger's mouth and there saw a sharp bone splinter stuck in the animal's throat.

"Oh, you poor thing!" the student said. "There's a bone stuck in you throat. Here, let me take it out.

Easy now, it will soon be better." The student stuck his hand into the tiger's mouth and gently pulled the bone out.

The tiger licked the student's hands and looked up into his face with tears of relief and gratitude, as if to say: "Thank you, thank you for your kindness." Then, bowing low many times, the tiger walked toward the woods, turning to look back from time and time at the student.

That night, as he slept, the student had a strange dream. A beautiful girl, whom he had never seen before, appeared in his sleep and said: "I am the tiger you saved today. Thanks to your gentle kindness, I was spared much pain and suffering. I shall surely show my gratitude to you some day." With that, the beautiful girl faded away.

Many years passed. The young student who had helped the tiger was now ready to take his final examinations in the capital city. As he rode along toward the capital he was thinking that if he passed these examinations he would become a government official and would one day become rich and famous. But many, many students came to take the tests from all over the country. In fact, there were so many

applicants that it was most difficult to pass the examinations.

The student prayed in his heart that he would be one of the fortunate ones to pass the difficult examinations. But it was not to be so. He failed. There were just too many people ahead of him.

The youth was very despondent. "I have come such a long, long way to the city. But I suppose it can't be helped; I'll return home, study hard, and try again next year." In this way he resigned himself to his failure and prepared to return to his home in the country the next day.

That night, however, the young student again had

a dream. Again the strange beautiful girl appeared and said: "Don't be discouraged. Keep your chin up. It's still too early to despair. I shall repay you for the kindness you showed me many, many years ago. Tomorrow a wild tiger will run loose through the city. That tiger will be myself. However, no gunman nor bowman will be able to kill me. I am sure the king will offer a big reward to anybody that succeeds in getting rid of me. At that time, make yourself known and offer your services. Just take one random shot at me. You will be sure to hit me."

The student was astounded to hear this and quickly replied: "No, no! I can't possibly do such a thing. Just because of one little kindness, I cannot take your life."

"No, you mustn't think that way," the tiger said, still in the form of a young woman. "I am very old and just about ready to die. I have very few days left to live. Since that's so, it's my wish to show you my gratitude. Don't say another word—just do as I have told you."

The student would not listen to the tiger. "But how can I do such a thing? I cannot commit such a cowardly act just to win fame for myself."

Suddenly the girl flared in anger. "Why can't you understand?" she said. "By saying such things you are spurning my sincere feelings of gratitude. Cease your talking and do just as I have told you. Oh, one more thing—a number of people will be hurt. Go then to the Temple of Hungryung and ask for some bean paste. If you apply this bean paste to the wounds of the people, they will soon be healed."

The girl repeated her instructions many times and then faded away from his dreams. It was then that the young student awoke.

The student pondered over the strange dream that he had had and waited in restless anticipation for the day to break. And, sure enough, as dawn broke a wild tiger appeared in the city and ran amok through the streets.

The capital was in an uproar. Bowmen and gunmen were dispatched to kill the tiger. But no matter how carefully they aimed their weapons, they could not hit the animal. The people were now in a terrible panic. Many had been hurt. Finally the king sent out a crier to announce a royal proclamation.

"Hear ye! Hear ye!" the crier cried. "The King

proclaims that anyone who shoots the tiger shall be greatly rewarded. A high court rank shall be bestowed upon him and a great treasure of rice shall be his."

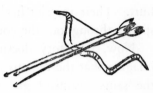

The student was surprised to hear this. A high court rank, and a treasure of rice—the rice alone would be enough to maintain a large retinue of retainers. And then he remembered the dream of the night before.

So the young student went before the king and said: "O King! I shall kill the tiger." The king gladly gave his consent for the student to hunt the rampaging animal.

The student went to the main street of the capital where the tiger was prowling about. Without even taking aim, the student took one shot at the animal. The wild tiger, that had the whole city in confusion, dropped dead.

That very day the student was made a nobleman and given his reward of a treasure of rice. Nor did the student forget about the bean paste from the Temple of Hungryung. He got the paste and applied it to the wounds of the people who had been hurt. Their injuries healed so quickly that his fame spread throughout the country.

Now, the story doesn't say so, but it is easy to imagine that the famous nobleman found for his wife the same beautiful girl whose shape the tiger had used in the young student's dreams—and that they lived together happily for many, many long years.

23 The Pumpkin Seeds

THERE once lived in the same village two brothers. The elder was greedy and miserly. The younger was a gentle and open-hearted man. The older brother lived in a great mansion and did not want for anything. Yet he was always complaining, as if by habit, that he led a hard life. On the other hand, his younger brother was poor and lived a humble life. But he never once complained.

One spring, swallows from some faraway southern country came and made a nest under the eaves of the poor brother's house. By the time the early summer breeze was rippling the green rice-seedlings, the swallow had hatched its eggs, and the nest was full of young birds. From morning to night, the baby birds made merry music under the eaves of the poor man's straw-thatched house. The kind-hearted younger brother placed a wide board under the nest to catch the baby birds, lest they fall from the nest to the ground below. The parent swallows busily carried food to the their young and worked hard to make them grow big. And they did grow big, with each passing day.

One day, while the parent birds were away looking for food, a large green snake slid down the roof of the hut. As it approached the swallow's nest, it raised its head and peered inside, as if to say: "Yum, yum! These young birds should make good eating." The snake poised itself to strike, showing its fangs. Of course, the baby swallows had never seen such a horrible sight before. They flapped their small wings in fear and tried with all their might to fly from this unexpected danger. But their wings were too weak. One little bird succeeded in taking off only to crash to the ground.

The young brother heard the commotion and came running out of the house. He saw the snake just in time and, with a great cry, chased it away.

The bird that had fallen from the nest had broken a leg. "Oh, you poor little thing," the brother said, "it must be painful." He gently lifted the bird from the ground, put medicine on its leg, and wound it carefully with a bit of white cloth.

Ten, twenty days passed. The baby swallow with the broken leg was soon well again. It was strong enough to fly now. It no longer needed to wait for its mother to bring it food. It swooped through the great sky, swiftly and freely, in search of insects and bugs.

Summer passed and autumn came. The swallows left for their winter home in the south. The swallow with the broken leg was now a big bird. Reluctantly, it too joined the migrating birds and left the village.

Early the next spring, the swallows came back to their old nest. They had travelled a long way, over seas and over mountains, but they had not forgotten their old home. The happy swallows swooped under the eaves of the straw-thatched hut. The humble hut of the younger brother again echoed to the merry chirping of birds.

The swallow that had broken its leg the year before also returned. As if to repay the young brother's kindness, it carried in its beak a pumpkin seed. The bird dropped the seed in a corner of the poor brother's yard, where it soon sprouted and shot forth a tendril that gradually climbed up to the roof of the poor man's home.

By autumn, three big pumpkins, so large that each made an armful, were ripening on the vine. The younger brother was overjoyed and cut down one pumpkin. "This is a rare thing to have such large pumpkins. One such pumpkin alone would be enongh to feed many people. I must take some of it to the villagers." So thinking, the young brother cut the pumpkin in two.

What should happen then! Out of the pumpkin trooped a host of carpenters. Some carried axes, some saws, some planes, and some hammers. Each carried some kind of tool. After the carpenters had all come out, there came a flow of building materials—timbers, planks, window frames, and doors. In a twinkling of an eye, the carpenters built a large mansion and then disappeared from sight.

The younger brother was completely dumbfounded at this strange and unexpected happening. He then began wondering what the other pumpkins might contain. He gingerly cut open the second pumpkin.

Out came a host of servants. There were farmhands too, with plows and spades and rakes. There were also maids, carrying water jugs on their heads, and seamstresses, with needles in their hands. When they had all come out, they lined up before the younger brother and, bowing deeply, said together: "Master, we are here to serve you. Please bid us as you desire."

From the third pumpkin there flowed silver and gold in such quantities that the younger brother was completely dazed. Overnight, he became the richest man in the village, and soon he was the owner of vast lands, purchased with the money that had come from the third pumpkin.

The greedy elder brother was green with envy. His every waking thought was how to become as rich as his younger brother. One day he came over to visit his brother, whom he had ignored for so long in the past. Slyly he asked: "Say, my dear brother, how did you manage to become so wealthy?"

The honest younger brother did not hide anything, but told everything that had happened.

The older brother, when he heard the story, could hardly bear his impatience. As soon as early summer came the next year, he took a baby swallow from one of the nests in his eaves and broke its leg. Then he put

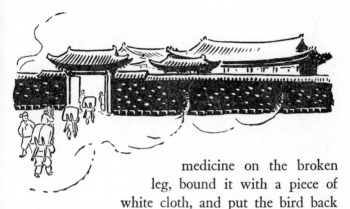

medicine on the broken
leg, bound it with a piece of
white cloth, and put the bird back
into its nest. In autumn this swallow flew away to
the south.

The older brother could scare contain his joy:
"I've only to wait a short while longer. Then that
swallow will return and bring me a pumpkin seed
too."

Sure enough, the swallow whose leg had been
broken on purpose returned the next spring to the
elder brother's house. And sure enough, it brought
back a pumpkin seed in its mouth.

The older brother took the seed and planted it in
a corner of his yard. Every day he gave it water and
cried: "Hurry and grow big! Hurry and grow big!"
He did not forget to mix a lot of manure into the

ground where the pumpkin seed had been planted.

In time, out came a green sprout. It grew and grew, stretching its vine up over the roof. In time, too, three pumpkins took shape and ripened. The pumpkins were much larger than those that had grown at his younger brother's house.

"How lucky I am!" the older brother said. "Thank Heaven! Now everything is set. I shall be much richer than my brother." He could not help dancing about in joy and anticipation.

Finally the time came and he cut the first pumpkin. But what should appear? Not carpenters, but a swarm of demons with cudgels in their hands.

"You inhuman and greedy monster! Now you'll get what you deserve!" the demons cried, and they began belaboring the older brother in turns.

After a while the demons disappeared. The older brother was all blue with bruises, but still he had not learned his lesson. "This time, for sure, I'll find much treasure," he thought, and cut open the second pumpkin.

But this time a host of money collectors came out, crying: "Pay your debts! Pay your debts! If you don't we'll take away everything we can lay our hands on."

And they did! They grabbed everything in sight. In a flash, the older brother's home was completely emptied of all it contained, leaving only a shell.

The older brother cursed himself for having cut open the second pumpkin, but it was too late. And still he could not give up his dreams of an easy fortune. He stuck a knife into the third pumpkin and split it open. What should come out but a flood of yellow muddy water. It came bubbling out in an unending stream. It flowed in such quantities that soon his home, his garden, and his fields were covered with yellow mud.

The older brother finally could stand it no longer. With a cry of anguish he fled to the shelter of his younger brother's house.

The kind-hearted younger brother greeted him with open arms and treated him with every consideration. The older brother suddenly realized how selfish and mean he had been. He became a humble and contrite man.

The younger brother gave his elder brother half of everything he had—paddies, fields, servants, and money—and from that time on the two lived on the most friendly of terms.

24 The Three Princesses

ONCE there was a king who had three daughters. All three of the princesses were gentle, noble, and beautiful. But of the three the youngest was regarded by all as the loveliest girl in the land.

One moonlit night the three princesses climbed a small hill behind their father's castle to view the beautiful moon. Suddenly, a huge eagle swept down as if from nowhere and, in a flash, snatched the three princesses up in its giant talons. Then it rose into the air and disappeared with the princesses.

The whole castle was thrown into turmoil. The king's bowmen and gunmen came rushing up the hill. But it was too late. The eagle was nowhere to be seen. All they could do was to gaze into the sky and bemoan the fate of the three girls.

The king's sorrow at losing all three of his daughters at one stroke was pitiful to behold. He immediately sent out his soldiers to proclaim throughout the land that anyone who succeeded in saving the three princesses would be given half his kingdom. In addition, he promised to give the savior of the girls his youngest and most beautiful daughter in marriage.

But who was there to save the princesses?

There was one, and only one, man in the whole country who knew where the maidens had been taken. He was a young warrior living deep in the mountains. This young man had left all human habitation behind and gone far into the mountain wilderness to perfect his martial skills. At night this solitary warrior used to mount his steed and practice with his spear and sword.

One night, as usual, the warrior had donned his armour and helmet and was spurring his steed in mock combat when he saw a huge eagle flying toward him. When it came near he saw, clutched in its talons, three young girls. By the light of the full moon, the warrior followed the flight of the great bird, and spurred his horse over hill and dale in pursuit. All night long he chased the giant bird and, near dawn, he saw the eagle alight at the base of a vast cliff and disappear from sight.

The warrior whipped his horse on, and after a time reached the spot at the base of the high cliff where the eagle had disappeared. Here he espied a hole in the base of the cliff. This, the warrior thought, must be was the entrance to the Land-below-the-earth, a place he had heard about only in rumors. After carefully studying the entrance, the warrior was certain that he was right.

The warrior had also heard that in the Land-below-the-earth there lived a terrible ogre who slept, once he fell asleep, for three months and ten days. This ogre had many henchmen and kept a large number of eagles, which he used to steal treasures and kidnap people from the earth above. The warrior marked with care the entrance to the Land-below-the-earth and returned to his lonely home.

By next morning the story of the disappearance of the three princesses and the king's proclamation had reached even this remote part of the mountains where the warrior was in training. The young man set off immediately for the king's palace and was received in audience.

"O King," the young man said, "I shall bring back the three princesses."

The king answered: "Please do whatever you can."

The young warrior then asked the king for the loan of the five strongest men among the king's soldiers. Then be began preparations for his venture into the Land-below-the-earth. He prepared a hempen rope a hundred leagues in length, a basket large enough to hold one person, and a silver bell. Then the young warrior set off for the mountains, accompanied by the five retainers.

After many days, he came once again to the entrance of the Land-below-the-earth. He tied the basket to one end of the hempen rope and at the other end the silver bell. His idea was to lower the basket by the rope, and when the bell was rung, to pull it up.

The warrior ordered one of the soldiers to go down in the basket first. The man had gone down only one league when the bell rang "Tinkle, tinkle." The man was hauled up to the surface. He was white with terror. A second soldier went down as far as five leagues, but he too became afraid and was pulled back. A third, and then a fourth, was sent down, but each was overcome with fear part way down and had to be hauled out. Even the strongest of the soldiers, the fifth man, could only go down fifty leagues.

Finally the young warrior himself entered the basket and was lowered into the hole. Down, down he went. There seemed no end. Just as the hundred-league rope ran out, the warrior touched bottom. He had finally reached the Land-below-the-earth!

There he found thousands of large and small houses lined up, row after row. Among them he noticed one that was larger than the rest. It stood without any roof. "This," he thought, "must be the home of the ogre." The young warrior racked his brains for some scheme by which he could enter

the house of the ogre, who was chief of the Land-below-the-earth.

As he approached the house, he noticed a well in the yard, and beside the well there stood a large willow tree. The warrior climbed up the tree and carefully hid himself in the branches. Then he waited to see what would take place.

Soon a young girl came to draw water from the well. She filled her jug with water and lifted it in both hands to place it on her head. Just then the young warrior plucked four or five of the willow leaves and let them flutter down. The leaves fell into the water which had just been drawn from the well. The young girl emptied the jar and drew fresh water from the well.

The warrior again dropped leaves into the jar. Again the girl threw the water out and refilled her container. Once again the leaves came fluttering down, and once again the girl emptied the jar and refilled it.

"My, what a strong wind!" she said, and glanced up into the tree. At the sight of the warrior hidden there, she was startled. "Are you not from the earth above? Why have you come to this place?" she asked.

The warrior then told her how the three princesses

had been kidnapped by a giant eagle and how he had been sent to save them.

The girl suddenly started to cry and said: "To tell you the truth, I am the youngest of the three princesses who were seized by the eagle. I was brought here with my two sisters. I had given up all hope of ever returning home. You cannot imagine how happy I am to see you. The ogre has just gone out. Once he sets out he does not return for three months and ten days. But, if we run away now, it would mean that the ogre would still be living, and, as long as he lives, he will try to steal us away again. You must wait until the ogre comes back and then get rid of him for good. But can you do that?"

"Yes," the warrior answered, "of course, I can. That's why I came all this way."

"I'm glad to hear that," the princess answered. "Come, I'll show you how to get into the ogre's house."

The youngest princess then led the young warrior to the ogre's house and hid him there in the store-house. In the storehouse there was a large iron pestle. The princess pointed to it and said: "Let me see how strong you are. Try and lift that pestle."

The young warrior grabbed the pestle with

both hands, but he couldn't budge it an inch.

"At that rate, you'll never be able to take the ogre's head," the princess said. She went into the ogre's house and returned with a bowlful of mandrake juice kept by the ogre, and told the young warrior to drink it. He drank the juice in one gulp, and when he grabbed the pestle again, he was able to move it just about an inch.

The young warrior stayed hidden in the store-house. Every day he drank mandrake juice and wrestled with the iron pestle. Day after day he practiced and tested his strength. Finally he was able to lift the iron pestle with one hand and fling it about as if it were a pair of chopsticks. But still the young warrior continued to drink the juice of the mandrake as he waited impatiently for the return of the ogre.

One day the ground began to tremble and the house to shake. The ogre had finally come home, together with his many henchmen. They brought with them many treasures which they had stolen. When they finished carrying their spoils into the house, they prepared a mighty banquet. That night, they feasted on delicacies of the mountains and the seas and quaffed wine by the barrelful. All night long they wined and danced, and the warrior watched them from a hiding place.

One by one the henchmen went to sleep, completely drunk. The ogre also finally toppled over in a drunken sleep. He lay snoring away.

"Now's my chance," the warrior thought and,

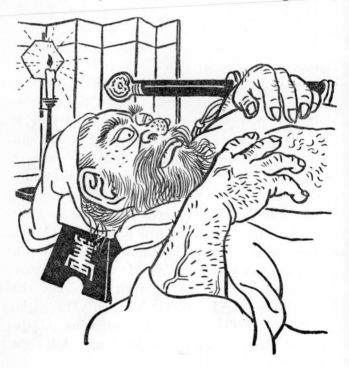

drawing his sword, crept up to the sleeping ogre. But imagine the warrior's surprise! The ogre lay with his eyes wide open, although he was snoring loudly.

The princess, who had followed the young warrior into the room, then said in a small voice: "You don't have to worry. The ogre always sleeps with his eyes open."

Then with a tremendous shout, the warrior slashed

with all his might at the ogre's neck. At this, the ogre jumped up, drew his sword, and tried to parry the blow. But the warrior's keen blade had already bitten deep into the ogre's neck, and he could not move as quickly as usual. Under the strength of the warrior's repeated blows, the ogre finally toppled over again. The warrior straddled the huge giant and finally succeeded in cutting off his head.

The severed head, however, bounded up and tried to attach itself to the bleeding neck. Just then the princess took out some fine ashes of burnt straw, which she had kept hidden under her dress, and threw them over the stump of the neck. The head let out one sad wail, then leaped up in one powerful jump, crashed through the ceiling, and disappeared.

The ogre's henchmen, when they learned what had befallen their chief, all surrendered meekly. The young warrior then threw open the many storehouses of the ogre, each filled to brimming with gold and silver, and divided up the treasure among the ogre's henchmen. Then he gathered together the three princesses and returned to the place where the basket had been lowered.

The warrior pulled at the hempen rope, ringing the bell at the other end. The king's soldiers, who had been waiting there all this time, began hauling away. One by one the princesses were pulled up to the earth above. At the very end, the warrior also came up safely.

The king was overjoyed at the return of his daughters. He ordered twenty-one days of celebration. The whole land also rejoiced at their salvation from the terrors of the ogre from the Land-below-the-earth.

The king did not forget his promise to the young warrior. He gave his youngest daughter, the most beautiful of the three princesses, to the warrior in marriage. He also gave the young man much land and wealth. The young warrior and his beautiful wife lived long and happily ever after.

25 The Disowned Student

LONG ago, there was once a young student. Now, it was the custom in those days for a student to go into the quiet of the mountains to some lonely temple and there spend his days in study in order to become a great scholar. So this young student left his home and went away to a mountain temple to read books and meditate for three long years. The days passed slowly at first. But one year passed, then two years, and in no time, the three years were at an end. The student had completed his studies and could now go home to his parents.

However, whom should he see upon his return? There was another young student in his home, identical to himself in appearance, speech, and manner.

What a surprise for the student to find someone just like himself! But what really troubled him was the fact that his own parents and his own brothers and sisters would not accept him as a member of the family. They treated him as if he were an imposter. He had come home after all these years, but they would not even let him enter the house.

"It's no joke," the young student said. "Can't you see I am your own son? I've just returned from the temple after studying for three years. This youth must be a bogey." Thus the young student pleaded with his parents and his brothers.

The other student, however, did not remain silent. He came out and shouted: "Be quiet, you imposter! You're just an old fox up to its trick of fooling people. Go away before we find you out."

That voice! It was the same as his own. It seemed impossible, yet even his own family could not tell the difference between the two. They looked the two youths over carefully. But the two students wore the same clothing. They even had the same birthmarks, the same scars. They were exactly alike. The parents then asked them about their birthdays and small details of their childhood and memories of any special occasion that might help solve the problem. But the two youths gave the same answers. As a last resort the parents then asked the two to name each article of furniture in the house, without leaving out an item.

Unfortunately, the real son had been away for three whole years, and he could not answer with ease. The other youth, however, had been living in the house for some time and was able to list everything without any trouble.

"Well, that decides it," the family said. "You are the imposter. Be on your way!" So saying, they finally drove their real son out of the house.

The poor youth was at a loss as to what to do. He knew it was useless to argue. He left home, still wondering what he should do. Day after day he continued his exile, wandering lonely here and there.

One day, he met a bonze who gazed kindly into his face and said: "You've had yourself stolen, haven't you? There is someone who looks exactly like you, isn't there?"

"Here's someone who may help me," thought the youth, surprised at the way the priest could read his troubles. So the youth opened up his heart and told the priest how he had returned home after three years of study only to find that another had taken his place in his home. He told also how he had been chased out by his family.

"H'm, h'm," the priest nodded, as he listened to the young student's tale. "Did you ever throw away the trimmings of your fingernails somewhere while you were studying at the temple?"

"Yes," the student answered, "there was a river

running right in front of the temple. I used to bathe in that river. Then after bathing, I would sit on the stones nearby and cut my nails. The trimmings I left on the stony river bank."

"Just as I thought," the priest said. "Whoever has eaten your fingernail trimmings has taken over your identity. Go straight home once again. But this time take a cat with you. Hide it in the sleeve of your robe so that none will know that you have it. When you get home, let the cat out right in front of the imposter. Then all will become known."

The student did as the priest told him. He hid a cat in his sleeve and returned home. His parents came out again. So did the imposter. But before they could say anything, the young student let the cat out, right in front of the person who had taken his place in the family.

The imposter suddenly turned white, and the cat pounced upon him and bit into his neck. There was a great struggle. In the end, the imposter fell to the ground, right in the middle of the room, his throat cut open by the cat's sharp teeth. The parents and the brothers and sisters looked carefully. There, to their surprise, lay not their son and brother, but a large field rat!

The rat had eaten the clippings of the young student's fingernails and had stolen the youth's identity. The spirit of human beings dwells in the fingernails. Thus, the rat who ate the student's fingernail clippings had been able to change readily into the shape of the young man. But a cat can smell a rat, no matter how disguised. And so, thanks to the bonze's wise advice, the story ends happily.

26   The Signal Flag

ONCE upon a time there was an old man who was totally blind. Although he could not see anything, he had a strange power. He could perceive things which ordinary people could not. For instance, he could see the evil spirits that enter the bodies of men and women, making them ill or even bringing about their deaths. Furthermore, the old man knew the secret of casting spells over the evil spirits to make them harmless. Time and time again, therefore, the old man had saved men and women from the evil spirits that tormented them. He had saved hundreds of people and was famous throughout the land.

One day the old man was walking down a road, feeling his way about, when he felt a messenger boy pass by. And there actually was a messenger boy walking past him, carrying a great number of cakes in a box strapped to his back. The old man could tell that a small devil was sitting in the box with the cakes. The evil spirit, of course, was invisible to everyone but the old man.

"That little devil!" the old man thought. "He's up to some mischief. He plans to go into some house and cause trouble." So saying, the old man followed the messenger down the road to a large house.

It was a house where a large wedding was being held. The boy entered the house and left the cakes that had been ordered for the wedding feast. The messenger then left after thanking the owners for their patronage.

The house was full of people, all in their fine clothes, gathered to celebrate this happy occasion. The old man waited outside to see what would happen.

Suddenly, there was a great commotion. The bride, who had been sitting in the inner room, had hardly taken a bite of one of the cakes when she fell to the ground and breathed her last. The evil spirit that had been sitting on the cakes had gone straight to the bride to do his mischief. The house was in an uproar, for, after all, one of the main figures in the wedding feast had passed away all of a sudden.

The old man immediately entered the house. "Don't worry," he said. "I shall save the bride for you."

The people immediately became quiet, for there was none who did not know of the old man's reputation. In fact, there were even some among the wedding guests who had been rescued themselves by him from evil spirits.

"The blind man is here! He can save the bride!" the guests cried joyfully. They were, indeed, so happy that it seemed as if the bride had already been restored to life.

Before the old man entered the bride's room to cast his spell over the evil spirit, he said to everyone present: "Close up all openings to the bride's chamber. Close the windows, the doors, the cracks, and the keyholes. Not a single hole, not even one as small as a pin-prick, must be left."

The people did exactly as the old man had said. They closed all doors and windows and pasted up any and all openings they could find. After everything was ready, the old man entered the room and began praying. From the room came the quiet murmur of the old man's incantation.

In no time, there arose the sound of loud banging from within the room. It was the devil, feeling the torturing effects of the old man's spell. It writhed and it groaned as it struggled like a crazed beast to resist the old man's magic power. The devil's anguish was terrible to hear. The people outside thought the old man and the devil were surely locked together in mortal combat.

But it was not so. The old man was simply sitting by the dead bride's side, with his hand on her forehead, intoning his curse in a low, quiet voice. The old man continued on and on, chanting out his spell, gradually pressing the evil spirit to the floor.

Now, there was one young servant in the house who was not very bright. He burned with curiosity as he listened to the noise coming from the bride's room. Finally, he could no longer restrain himself. He crept up to the room and made a wee hole in the paper-covered sliding door—a hole so small that only a needle would go in. Then the young servant peeked in.

But the devil had been waiting for something like this to happen. He saw his chance and, in a flash, slipped through the pinpoint hole and fled.

With the evil spirit gone, the bride came back

to life and was greeted with joy by the wedding guests.

But the old man was deathly white. He sighed and said: "Oh, what a terrible thing has happened! In just a little while I could have completed my spell, and the devil would have become harmless. But now the evil spirit is still at large. He is certain to revenge himself upon me. I haven't much longer to live."

The parents and the wedding guests were over-joyed to see the bride alive again. Forgetting the old man, they crowded about her, all trying to say how happy they were. In all this great fuss, the old man left the house before anyone had even thanked him properly.

The old man's reputation became greater and

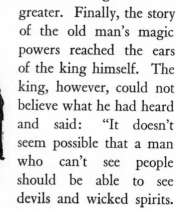

greater. Finally, the story of the old man's magic powers reached the ears of the king himself. The king, however, could not believe what he had heard and said: "It doesn't seem possible that a man who can't see people should be able to see devils and wicked spirits.

He must surely be using some evil magic and fooling the people." The king then called his men and ordered them to bring the blind man before him.

When the old man appeared, the king placed a dead mouse before him and said: "Try and guess what I have placed in front of you."

"Yes, I shall. There are three mice there," the blind man replied.

"You'd be right," the king said, "if you said a mouse, but why do you say three mice?"

"I am certain that there are three mice," the old man countered. "There is no mistake about that."

"Quiet!" the king roared in anger. "There is only one mouse here. Are you trying to say that there is more than one mouse when I see only one with my good eyes?"

The king could not contain his anger and sternly continued: "You have fooled many people. You have committed a grave crime. In punishment, I sentence you to the extreme penalty. You shall have your head chopped off."

So the old man was handed over to the executioners and carried away immediately to the place of execution, which lay on the outskirts of the city.

After the king had handed the old man over to

his death, he stopped and wondered: "He was able to tell that it was a mouse right away. Maybe it's not entirely false about his being able to see evil spirits. But I wonder why he insisted there were three mice instead of one?" The king, out of curiosity, had the mouse cut open. There to his surprise, he saw two small baby mice inside.

"This is terrible!" the king shouted. "Hurry and stop that execution!"

A retainer climbed the high castle tower and there unfurled the signal flag. Now, it was the custom for the executioners, before cutting off a criminal's head, to confirm the sentence by looking at this signal flag on the castle tower. If the flagpole leaned to the right, it meant the criminal had been pardoned. If the flagpole inclined to the left, the execution was to be carried out as ordered.

The retainer lifted the flagpole and slanted it to the right. Just then, a sudden, strong gust of wind pushed the flagpole to the left. So strong was the wind that no matter how hard he tried, the retainer could not push the pole sideways to the right. The executioners, not knowing of this struggle, saw only that the flagpole was leaning to the left. Without further ado, they executed the poor blind man.

Just then, there was strange, crackling laugh near the flagpole on the castle tower. It came from the wicked spirit that had so narrowly escaped the old man's spell. He had taken his revenge!

27   The Magic Hood

THERE once lived a man who held his ancestors in great honor. The custom of the country was to have the names of the family's ancestors inscribed on votive tablets which were reverently set up in the family shrine. Then, whenever an anniversary of the death of one of the ancestors came about, the family would offer good food to the spirits of the dead and hold a ceremony in their memory.

Now, this man had one great weakness. He could not rest content unless his memorial ceremonies were more lavish than those of his neighbors. His weakness was to have so many different dishes of meat, fowl, and fish that they could not all be placed on the table set before the votive tablets in front of the family shrine in the main room of the house.

The little goblins, who knew this man's weakness, decided one day to come and eat up the feasts the man would prepare for his ancestors. Each of the goblins had a magic hood which, when worn, made him invisible to men's eyes. The next memorial day, the goblins came in their magic hoods and ate up all the delicacies the man had prepared. From that day on, whenever the man prepared a feast in honor of his ancestors, the goblins were sure to be there.

Of course, the man did not know what the goblins were doing. He was simply happy that his deceased ancestors were apparently enjoyng their feasts so much. As this continued, the man began to increase the quantity of food and the number of dishes. But no matter how much food he prepared, it always disappeared overnight.

Finally, the man realized that even dead ancestors could hardly eat all that much. "There is something funny about this," he thought. The next time a memorial event came along, the man as usual set out many dishes on a table and placed it before the votive tablets. Then he got a long stick and hid behind a screen.

The hours passed slowly. It was the dead of night. Suddenly, the food started to disappear from the heaped platters set on the table. He listened carefully. From somewhere came the sound of eating and drinking. The man jumped out from behind the screen and started slashing the air above the table with his long stick.

The goblins were taken completely by surprise. They ran helter-skelter from the room. One of the goblins, however, could not dodge the stick fast enough. The end of the long stick caught a corner of his magic hood and lifted it from its head.

The man was surprised to see a red hood come falling from nowhere to the floor. He picked it up and placed it on his head and cried: "Robbers! Help! Help!"

His wife, who had been sleeping all this while, came running in great haste into the room. But nowhere was her husband to be seen.

When the man saw the puzzled expression on his wife's face, he said: "The little goblins dropped this funny red hood."

But still the wife could not see her husband and looked around the room in bewilderment. The man went right up to his wife and then took off the hood.

To her surprise, her husband suddenly appeared out of thin air and stood right in front of her.

The wife looked at the funny red hood which her husband showed her. Out of curiosity, she put it on her head. She too disappeared from sight. For the first time, the two realized the magic virtues of the red hood.

"This is a wonderful thing we have gotten hold of," the man said. And, from that day, he often put the hood on and went out to rob people in their homes. He took anything and everything that pleased him. He stole many, many things from many, many homes.

One whole year passed in this manner. One day the man put on his red hood and went into a merchant's home. The merchant was in his inner room counting out silver and gold pieces.

Suddenly, the gold and silver pieces began disappearing one by one before the merchant's very eyes. "This is impossible!" the merchant cried. "It cannot be!"

Then he looked around the room. There, right in front of his eyes, he saw a small, thin strand of red thread dangling from nowhere, swaying back and forth. The man had used the cap so often that it had become ragged and had started to unravel.

The merchant quickly caught the thread and tugged at it. Off came the hood from the man's head, and there he was, completely visible to the surprised merchant. The merchant pounced on the man and dealt him many blows. Then, after taking the magic hood away from him, he chased the man from his house.

The merchant then sewed up the ragged edges of the magic hood and, just as the other man had done,

started wearing it to go out and steal.

One day he slipped into the house of a wealthy farmer. It was harvest time. The threshers were busy in the yard threshing the new wheat. The merchant picked his way carefully through the threshers. But, by chance, the end of one of the flails, lifted in mid-air, caught the corner of his hood. Off it came, and the merchant was exposed to the full view of the threshers. The merchant was thrown into a panic and made a dash for freedom across the threshing floor. But the threshers, completely occupied with their work, kept flailing away, not even noticing the merchant. The merchant in his mad dash was hit on the head time and time again, until he fell unconscious to the floor.

The magic hood, which had dropped to the ground, was stepped on by this man and that. It was kicked about and crushed by so many feet that it soon became nothing but a dirty red rag, torn to shreds. And finally it disappeared altogether.

That was the end of the magic hood of the little goblin.

The Father's Legacy

ONCE there lived an old man who had three sons. In time he grew very, very old and lay on his death-bed. Just before he drew his last breath, he called his sons to his bedside.

"You have cared for me a long time," he told them. "I have only a few more minutes left to live. I want to give each of you a legacy, but, unlike in the old days, we now live in such poverty that I have nothing of value to leave to you. However, I want to leave at least something for you. When I die, you must must leave this unfortunate house and try to find your own fortunes by yourselves." So saying, the old man bequeathed the eldest brother a stone-mill. To his second son he left a long bamboo cane and a wine jug made from a gourd. And to the youngest son he left a hand-drum.

Soon, the old man passed away. The three sons wept sorely at their father's death, but they did not forget to give him a decent burial. Then, when the funeral was finished, they left home, each taking with him the legacy left him by his father.

After a while they came to a place where the road split into three. The three brothers promised each other that they would meet once again at this point on a certain day and then parted. The oldest brother took the road leading to the right, the second brother took the middle road, and the youngest proceeded along the road leading to the left.

The oldest brother, carrying the heavy stone-mill on his back, walked on and on. As the road started climbing into the mountains, night fell. It was a lonely section of the country, where almost nobody ever came. The brother was hungry. On top of that, a cold wind had started blowing. He did not have the strength nor the courage to continue on.

"I wonder if there's some place where I can sleep," the brother thought. Just then he spied an old tree standing just ahead. He decided he would spend the night under the tree and carried his heavy stone-mill there. However, he suddenly felt afraid.

"This is such a lonely place. What if some wild animal comes out at night?" he thought. He then again shouldered the stone-mill, which he had placed on the ground, and climbed with it up into the branches of the tree. There he hung the mill on a stout branch and settled himself to go to sleep.

It became completely dark. The night hours gradually passed. Tired from his long journey, the man was sound asleep. Suddenly he woke with a start. He could hear the sound of men talking

nearby. Startled, the brother sat up in the tree and thought:

"What in the world could he happening in this lonely place, so for from any houses?" He peered down into the darkness and listened closely.

There, underneath the tree, he could just make out a band of robbers arguing over the sharing of the goods they had stolen that day.

"Your share is too large!" said one.

"No, my share is not enough!" said another.

Then they started to count their money. The older brother was amazed to hear the men counting in large sums: "One thousand *ryang*. Two thousand *ryang*."

The brother suddenly nodded his head as though he had hit upon a good idea. He drew his stone-mill to him and started to grind away. The stones began making a noise like thunder.

The robbers under the tree were startled out of their wits. "This is terrible! There's not a single cloud in the sky, but it's thundering. The heavens are angry with us. We shall be punished. Let's go! Let's go!"

So saying, the robbers scattered helter-skelter, leaving behind them the gold and the silver and the treasures that they had stolen. The oldest brother climbed down from his perch in the tree and gathered up the spoils the robbers had left.

In this way, thanks to the stone-mill, the oldest brother became a rich man overnight and wasted no time in setting himself up in a splendid mansion.

The second brother walked on and on for days and days. One evening he passed by a lonely cemetery. Night had fallen and it was pitch-black. There wasn't a single star to be seen shining in the sky. The brother sat down beside a gravestone to rest his weary body, and waited for dawn to break.

It was just midnight when the brother heard the sound of footsteps from the other side of the dark graveyard. The footsteps sounded louder and louder as if the person were coming closer. It was so dark he couldn't make out who it was. He was so scared that he hardly dared to breathe and crouched against the gravestone, making himself as small as he could. The footsteps came right up the place where he leaned close to the stone.

"Hurry, hurry, Mr. Skeleton!" a voice said. "Get up! We have to do one job before dawn breaks. Tonight we're going to the home of a millionaire and steal his daughter's soul. Don't be such a lie-abed. Hurry and get up!" It was an evil spirit who had come.

When the brother heard the spirit's voice, he made up his mind in a flash and answered: "I've been awake for some time. Let's go then."

The evil spirit, hearing a strange voice, said in

a puzzled voice: "Say, you sound like a human being. Are you really a skeleton?"

"If you don't believe me," the brother said, "then feel me."

The evil spirit stretched out his hands and groped in the dark. "All right then," the spirit said, "let me feel your face."

The young man thrust forward the gourd wine jug that his father had given him. The spirit felt the jug and said: "You're right! Your head hasn't a single hair on it. You must be a skeleton. But to make sure let me feel your arm too."

The second son then put forth the long bamboo cane his father had left him. The spirit felt the bamboo cane and said: "What thin bones you have! How dry they are! A long, long time must have passed since you died." Then the spirit added: "Hurry! Let's go! It will soon be dawn."

The spirit and the brother walked quickly out of

the graveyard and set off straight for the millionaire's mansion. When they got there, the house was in complete darkness. Not a person was awake. The spirit left the younger brother at the gate, saying: "Listen, Mr. Skeleton! You wait here. I'll go in by myself and steal the daughter's soul."

So saying, the spirit slipped into the darkened mansion. A little while later, the spirit returned.

"Say, did you get the daughter's soul?" asked the brother.

"Of course," the spirit replied, "I plucked it right out of her. Here, I have it tightly held in my hand. This is the girl's soul."

"Why keep it in your hand? Put it in here," the second son said, hurriedly taking his draw-string purse from his belt.

The spirit put the soul into the purse and said: "Be careful now! Keep the purse tightly closed or the soul will escape."

The two then left the mansion and headed for the graveyard. Suddenly, away in the distance, they heard the first crowing of a cock.

The spirit started with surprise when he heard the crowing. "This is bad," he said and ran swiftly away, back to the place where spirits stay in the daytime, when they must not expose themselves.

When day broke and the red sun showed itself in the east, the brother returned to the gate of the millionaire's mansion. He could hear the sound of people crying. The whole house was in an uproar.

"Did something happen?" the brother asked innocently.

One of the servants replied: "The daughter of the house suddenly passed away in her sleep last night. She had never been sick in her life and so, when she died suddenly, everybody was shocked beyond belief."

"Perhaps I can bring the girl back to life," the brother said in a most innocent manner.

The servant, on hearing this, ran into the mansion. Soon the rich father came out to the gate and asked the young man in. "If you can really bring my daughter back to life, I will give you anything you desire. Please come have a look at my dead daughter," the father pleaded.

The old man then lead the second son to an inner room, where the body of the daughter lay. The second son waved everybody away and commanded that no one enter the room. Then he shut the doors and the sliding windows tightly so that none could look in. Then he went and sat beside the girl's body.

He took his purse out and, placing it close to the girl's nose, unloosened the purse strings.

The girl, who had not been breathing till then, suddenly turned over in her sleep. "My, I've over-slept," she said and opened her big, beautiful eyes.

The millionaire's mansion, which up till then had been filled with wailing voices, suddenly resounded with rejoicing. The father thanked the brother with tears of gratitude in his eyes. He bowed to the floor and kissed the young man's feet and said: "You are the savior of my daughter's life. No matter what I give you, I cannot repay you for what you have done. I believe you and my daughter must have been foreordained for each other from a previous life. I hope you will not take offense, but please take my daughter to be your wife."

The second son from that day on lived in the millionaire's mansion, as requested by the rich father. On an auspicious day picked by the soothsayers, the young man and the beautiful daughter were married. No man could be more fortunate than the second son, for not only did he win a beauteous and virtuous wife but he also received half the millionaire's wealth.

Thanks to his father's legacy, the second son was thus elevated in one day from poverty to wealth.

Meanwhile, what had happened to the youngest son?

Carrying the hand-drum left to him by his father, this brother walked on down the road leading to the left. By nature he was a carefree, happy-go-lucky man. He did not feel at all lonely, separated from his brothers. He travelled on and on for many, many days, until finally he saw in the distance a village set beside a beautiful forest.

His travels had not been in the least easy, but when he saw the beautiful scenery, he felt a strange feeling of elation. The brother started humming a song all to himself as he passed along a lonely path leading through the fields toward the village. He took down his hand-drum and began beating it in time to the tune he was humming. Then, caught in the rhythm of the drum he himself was beating, the young man started singing a song at the top of his voice as he walked on.

Suddenly, there appeared from the woods a large yellow animal which seemed to jog along in time to the song the youngest brother was singing. The young man looked closely, and, to his surprise, he saw that it was a huge tiger. Of course the young man was scared, but he kept right on singing and beating his drum. Soon, his fear disappeared as he watched the amusing way the tiger danced. The young man beat even more loudly on his drum. The tiger seemed overjoyed. It lifted its front paws off the ground and came dancing upright after the brother. The young man kept right on singing and beating away. The tiger kept following him, dancing to the beat of the drum. On and on the two danced, drawing closer and closer to the mountain village.

When the villagers saw the huge tiger dancing behind the young man, they all said: "This is a wonderful spectacle, the like of which we have never seen." And, one and all, they threw money at the young man.

The young man saw what was happening, and he added a new verse to his song:

> *Come everbody, come one and all,*
> *Listen and heed to this my call.*
> *Come see a tiger dance and prance—*
> *This is for you a lifetime's chance!*

After that, everywhere the young man went with his tiger great crowds gathered to see the marvellous sight of the dancing beast, and money poured into the young man's pockets.

Eventually the story of the young man reached

the ears of the king him-
self. The king said: "I
must see, at least once, a
tiger dancing to music.
Go and bring the young
man here."

The young man was
led into the presence of
the king, still playing his
drum and still singing,
with the tiger, of course,
following him. When
the king actually saw the
dancing tiger, which he

had only heard about till then, he could not help
wanting the animal for himself.

"I shall pay you any amount you name," the king
said to the young man. "Sell me that animal and
drum."

"No," the youngest brother replied, "this is a
treasure that has been handed down to me by my
ancestors. No matter how much money you pay
me, I cannot part with this my drum. And without
it the tiger won't dance."

In this way the young man declined the king's

growing offers many, many times. But, after all, a king is a king, and in the end the young man could not keep on refusing. So he finally agreed to sell the tiger and the hand-drum for the princely sum of ten thousand *ryang*.

Thus the youngest son also came into great wealth, thanks to his father's dying gift.

On the day the three brothers had promised to meet, they gathered once again at the fork of the three roads. They told each other of their hardships and of the wealth they had achieved. When each had told his story, the three brothers praised their father for the precious legacies he had left them. Each was now so wealthy that he had no reason to envy his brothers, and they lived on in happy fraternity for many, many years.

29 The Tiger of the Kumgang Mountains

THERE once lived a very famous marksman and hunter. He was such a fine marksman that he could shoot down any bird in flight, almost without taking aim. Deer and wild boar were no match for this hunter once they entered the sights of his gun. He was never known to have missed anything.

In those days the Kumgang Mountains were full of tigers. Often the beasts would come down from the fastnesses and steal, not only horses and cattle, but even human beings. But there was not a single man who could conquer the tigers. Many hunters had said, "I'll get those tigers," and had set out. But none had ever returned. Instead they had become the prey of the tigers of the Kumgang Mountains.

One day, the famous marksman said: "Now it's my turn. I shall kill every tiger in the mountains." The hunter, so saying, set out, refusing to listen to those who tried to hold him back.

The proud hunter went on and on. At the foot of the mountains he came to a lonely inn. The proprietress of the inn saw the hunter and said: "Alas, are you also going to the tigers to have them eat you up? Listen to what I say. It is for your good that I tell you. If you value your life, give up your foolish idea."

However, the hunter refused to listen. In his heart, he said proudly: "What with my skill, there isn't a tiger anywhere that can beat me."

Out loud, the hunter said to the woman: "Old woman, just wait and see. I shall come back in a little while, carrying a tiger as big as a mountain on my back." And, laughing to himself, the hunter continued up into the mountains.

That was the last ever seen of him. Five years passed. Ten years went by. But the hunter did not return.

When the hunter left home, he left behind a male child who had just been born. Now he had grown into a young lad, skilled with the gun. In fact he had become almost as good a marksman as his father. The young man knew well the reason why he was fatherless. He had long ago decided in his heart that he himself would shoot down the tiger that had eaten his father.

When he reached his fifteenth birthday, the boy went to his mother and said: "I would like to set out for the Kumgang Mountains. Mother, please let me go."

But the mother did not want to lose her son. With tears in her eyes, she tried to stop him: "Even a famous marksman like your father was eaten by the tigers. How can you avenge your father's death? If you go, you will never return. That is as clear as daylight. Quit thinking about such things and stay forever by your mother's side."

"Don't worry, Mother. I shall surely find the tiger who ate my father. I shall shoot it down and avenge his death." And the son earnestly begged his mother to let him go.

Finally the mother said: "If you want to go so much, do as you wish. But first let me ask you one thing. Your father used to have me stand with a water jug on my head. Then he would aim at the handle of the water jug from a distance of one league and shoot off only the handle without spilling any water. Can you do the same thing?"

When he heard this, the young son immediately tried to match his father's feat. He had his mother stand one whole league away, with a water jug on her head. He took careful aim, but he missed the mark entirely. So he gave up his idea of going to the mountains and practiced three more years with his gun.

After three years, he tried again. This time he succeeded in knocking off the handle of the water jug on his mother's head without spilling a drop of water.

Then the mother said: "Son, your father was able to shoot the eye out of a needle from a distance of one league. Can you do this?"

The son asked his mother to stand with a needle in her outstretched hand. Then he walked back a distance of one league and, taking careful aim, let go a shot. But he failed to shoot the eye out of the needle. Once again, he gave up his idea of going to the Kumgang Mountains and settled down to another three years of practicing.

At the end of three years, he again tried the same

trick. This time, with the crack of his gun, the eye of the needle fell to the ground.

Of course, what the mother had told her son were all lies. The mother had thought that if she told him such tales about his father, he would give up his idea of going to avenge his father. But her son had now successfully performed each of the feats she ascribed to her husband. Even the mother could not help being moved by her son's single-minded desire to avenge his father's death, and she finally gave him permission to leave for the Kumgang Mountains.

The son was overjoyed. He immediately set out for the mountains. At the foothills he came across the same small inn where his father had stopped years ago. The same old woman was still living. The old woman asked the young man what he intended to do. He told her how his father had been eaten by the tigers and how he had practiced for years to avenge his death.

The old woman then said: "Yes, I knew your father. He was the greatest marksman in all the land. Can you see that tall tree over in the distance? Why, your father used to turn his back to that tree and then shoot down the highest leaf on the highest branch from over his shoulder. If you can't do the same thing, how can you expect to avenge his death?"

The hunter's son, when he heard this, said he also would try. He placed his gun over his shoulder and took aim and shot. But he missed. He knew then that this wouldn't do, and he asked the old woman to let him stay with her a while. From that day, he kept practicing shooting over his shoulder at the tree. Finally, after three years had passed, he was able to shoot down the highest leaf on the highest branch.

Again the old woman told the hunter's son: "Just because you can do that, it still does not mean you can outshoot your father. Why, your father used to set an ant on the side of a cliff and then, from a

distance of one league, shoot that ant off without even scratching the surface of the cliff. No matter what a fine marksman you may be, you can't match that."

The young man then tried to do what the old woman said his father had done. Again he failed at first and had to practice three more years before succeeding.

Of course, all that the old woman had told him had been made up because she wanted to save the man. But the hunter's son, not questioning her once, had practiced till he could do whatever she said his father had done. The old woman was filled with amazement and admiration.

"It's safe now. With your skill, you will surely avenge your father's death." So saying, the old woman made many balls of cooked rice for him to eat along the way.

The hunter's son thanked her sincerely and started out along the path leading into the heart of the Kumgang Mountains.

Eating as he went the rice-balls made for him by the old woman, the young man pressed deeper and deeper into the mountains. For days and days he wandered through the wilderness. After all, the

Kumgang Mountains have twelve thousand peaks and stretch over a vast area, and he had no means of knowing where the tiger lay hidden. In this heart he kept praying that he would be able to find the tiger that had eaten his father, and he continued wandering, without any exact destination, through the vast mountain ranges.

One day, while the hunter's son was seated on a big rock taking a rest, a lone priest came up to him and asked: "Excuse me, sir. If you have a flint and stone, may I borrow it?"

The hunter's son brought out his flint and stone from the leather purse hanging from his belt and handed it to the priest. The priest struck fire with the flint and stone and lighted his tobacco pipe. As he opened his mouth to take the first puff, the young man caught a glimpse inside the priest's mouth. There he saw sharp fangs such as tigers have.

"Human beings don't have such fangs. He must be a tiger in disguise," the young man thought, and, without letting the priest see, he picked up his gun. "But what if he really is a man?" the young man pondered. He hesitated for a moment or two but suddenly felt sure of his suspicion and, raising his gun, let loose a shot at the priest's breast.

With a cry, the priest fell to the ground. When the young man looked down, there, instead of a priest lay the dead body of a huge tiger.

After making sure the tiger was quite dead, the hunter's son continued along the mountain trail. In a little while he came to an old woman digging potatoes in her potato patch. Since the young man was hungry, he asked: "Old woman, please give me one potato."

"I haven't any time to waste," the old woman replied. "My husband was just killed by a bad man. His soul just came to me and said that I must hurry and dig up some potatoes and take them to him to eat. Once he eats these potatoes he will become alive again. That's why I have to hurry."

"That's funny," the young man thought, and he looked carefully at the hands of the woman digging potatoes. He saw, not human hands, but the hairy paws of a tiger. The hunter's son immediately lifted his gun and took aim. "Bang!" went the gun, and the old woman in the potato patch toppled over and turned into an old she-tiger.

The hunter's son continued on his way. In a short while he came upon a young girl carrying a water jug balanced on her head. The young man was thirsty and asked: "Please kindly give me a drink of water."

The young girl answered: "I'm sorry, but I can't stop. I'm in a terrible hurry. The souls of my father-in-law and mother-in-law came to me and said they have been killed by an evil person and asked me to bring them water. I must hurry with this water and give it to them so they can come alive again."

So saying, the girl started hurrying on. From the front she was surely a young girl, but from behind she was tiger with a long tail. The hunter's son raised his gun and let fly a shot. Down came, not a girl, but a young she-tiger.

The hunter's son continued on. Down the road he saw a young man walking hurriedly toward him. The hunter's son called: "Say, won't you sit down with me? Let's exchange talk of our travels."

"No, I can't waste any time. My parents and my wife just came to me in a dream and told me that they have been shot down by a bad man. They asked me to come and offer sacrifices for them. If I delay longer, it'll be too late for them to come alive."

This young man too had a long tail hanging behind him. The hunter's son immediately raised his gun and shot the man dead. By the time the man's body hit the ground it had changed into a splendid young tiger.

The hunter's son was pleased with himself for having got rid of four tigers in such a short time. He felt greatly encouraged and continued on his journey, wondering what next lay in store for him. After a short while he saw a huge white animal, as big as a mountain, squatting in the distance. It was a huge, huge grandfather tiger that must have been alive for a thousand years.

The white-haired grandfather tiger opened its great

mouth to swallow the hunter. The young man quickly took aim and shot a bullet at the tiger's mouth. But the tiger did not even blink. The young man kept shooting one shot after another at the tiger. But, each time, the grandfather tiger would clench his teeth, draw back his lips, and let the bullets bounce off his fangs harmlessly. Undaunted, the young man kept shooting at the tiger. But, in the end, he ran out of bullets, and was swallowed in one gulp, gun and all, by the great grandfather tiger.

The tiger's throat was one black tunnel. Once the hunter had passed through this tunnel, he came to a vast room as large as a fairground. This was the giant tiger's stomach. The hunter was surprised to see scattered here and there the bones of people the tiger had eaten. He wondered whether he might not be able to find the bones of his father and started searching here and there. Just as he had thought, he found his father's bones beside a hunting rifle on which his father's name was engraved. The son carefully gathered the bones together and lovingly placed them in the bag at his belt.

Then the young man continued his search. He came upon an unconscious girl who lay huddled in a heap. The young hunter took the girl in his arms and nursed her back to consciousness. She looked into his face and thanked him with gratitude. She then revealed that she was the daughter of the king's minister, who was famous in the capital. The young girl told him how the old grandfather tiger had stolen her away, just the night before, while she was washing her hair on the verandah of her home.

The two talked over their plight and decided to join forces in finding a way out of the tiger's stomach. The young hunter took a knife from his belt and cut a small hole near the tiger's tail. Through it they could see outside. They decided that the girl should stay beside the hole and tell the young man whether the tiger was walking through a field, or up some craggy cliff, or along the seashore. The hunter's son then started cutting through the walls of the tiger's stomach. Because the stomach wall was so thick, he could not make much progress with his small knife. He cut with all his might and main and slowly started widening the cut that he had started.

The tiger at first bore his stomach pains. But as the pains increased, he could no longer keep still. He went to his doctor friend, an old bear, and said: "My stomach pains me terribly. Haven't you any good medicine?"

The bear answered: "That's nothing to worry about. Just eat a lot of fruit and you'll soon be well."

The tiger then started eating apples and pears right and left. The tiger's stomach became like one great fruit market. After all, being the huge animal that he was, the grandfather tiger was not content to eat only one hundred or two hundred apples or pears. He simply went into orchards and uprooted whole trees. The young girl and the man joyfully plucked the fruit from the trees swallowed whole by the tiger and filled their own stomachs. Now that they had eaten, they felt much stronger and took courage. With redoubled zeal the young man fell to his work of cutting away the tiger's stomach.

No matter how much fruit he ate, the tiger continued to feel greater and greater pains in his stomach. He again went to see the bear.

"I don't feel well at all. The pains in my stomach seem to be even worse than before."

The bear then said: "Go to the mineral spring and drink the water there. It's good for stomachaches."

The giant grandfather tiger went to the spring and gulped down great volumes of water. The young man and the girl in the tiger's stomach drank the clear sweet water and felt greatly refreshed. The young hunter again redoubled his efforts and kept slashing furiously away at the tiger's stomach.

Soon the tiger could no longer stand the pain in his stomach. He ran around like a crazed animal.

He jumped from high cliffs, and ran blindly through forests, knocking himself against rocks and trees. But no matter how he writhed and twisted, he could not get rid of the pain. Finally, even the grandfather tiger came to the end of his strength and stopped moving.

The young girl peeked out from her hole and found that they were by good fortune in the middle of a large field. She ran to the young man and helped him rip open the last remaining bit of flesh separating them from freedom. They then stepped outside safe and sound.

The young man skinned the tiger, for he wanted to take home the beautiful white tiger-skin as a present. Then, taking the young girl by the hand, he returned to his home, where his mother was waiting for him. His mother cried with tears of joy to see her son come back safely.

After burying the bones of his father in the family graveyard, the young hunter took the young girl back to her home in the capital city. Words cannot describe the joy the king's minister felt when he saw his daughter, returned home safe and sound. In gratitude the king's minister adopted the young hunter into his family to become his daughter's husband and to be heir to his name and fortune.

The young man returned to fetch his mother and the old woman of the mountain inn. And the whole family lived together happily ever after in the mansion of the king's minister.

30 The Silver Spoon

THE only son of a wealthy family had a tutor to help him in his studies. The tutor was a fine scholar, but he had only one eye and his nose was somewhat crooked. Because of this the servants of the house continually made fun of him. Even the food which the servants brought to him morning and night was not like that served the others. When he asked for anything, the servants would pretend they had not heard him. He would have to ask two or three times before the servants would do his bidding. The tutor was greatly troubled by the way the servants treated him.

But even more troubled was the young man of the house, the tutor's pupil. "I can't bear to see my tutor made fun of like this," he thought. "I've thought of a plan that will teach the servants a good lesson." The young master slipped quietly into the kitchen, so as not to be seen by the servants, and took from the kitchen cupboard his father's favorite silver spoon.

Next morning the servants were in an uproar. The kitchen maids were white with fear. What would happen to them if the master were to learn of the loss of the spoon? The servants consulted a witch. They also went to see a fortuneteller, to see if he might not tell them what had happened to the spoon and where it could be found. But neither witch nor fortuneteller were of any help. The servants searched high and low. The house was a welter of confusion.

The young son, with the most innocent expression on his face, casually asked one of the servants: "What's the matter? Everybody seems so upset this morning."

"Upset is not the word. The master's silver spoon is missing."

The youth suppressed his laughter and said: "Why, what a terrible thing! I wonder what could have happened to it?"

"If we knew, we wouldn't be in such a state now."

"That is bad." The youth was quiet for a while, as if in deep thought. Then he suddenly brightened, as if struck by a good idea, and said: "Hah! I know! My tutor is an amazing fortuneteller. He would surely be able to help you."

The servants had always made fun of the one-eyed, crooked-nosed tutor, but now they could do nothing in their plight but go ask him for help. The servants then did as the young master suggested.

First they served the tutor a special dinner with wine and the best of food to put the tutor in a good mood. Then the chief servant said: "The master's silver spoon has disappeared. Will you tell us where it is to be found?"

"What? You say a spoon has been lost? H'm..." The tutor cocked his head in thought, while he plied the wine glass to his lips in pleasure.

"Please," the servant implored, "you must help us! I am sure you can help us." And he bowed humbly many times before the tutor.

"Wait, wait. I shall try," the tutor said condescendingly. He sat down before his desk and pretended to be reading the future. After a while, he said confidently: "Well, well. The spoon is hidden quite near the house. Yes, it is under a stone that lies in a southeasterly direction. Let's see. A stone to the southeast? That must be the stones beside the well. Yes, that's it. If you look under the stones by the well, I am sure the spoon will be found."

The servants immediately went to the wellside and searched under all the stones. And there, sure enough, was the silver spoon. Of course, the spoon was found

there. Everything had been planned long in advance by the youth. He himself had taken the spoon and hidden it under the well-stones. He had, of course, told the tutor of his scheme and where the spoon had been hidden.

But the servants knew nothing of this scheming. Thus they naturally came to regard the tutor as a superior being. The servants, who up till then had been making fun of the tutor behind his back, now suddenly changed and began treating him with great respect. When mealtime came, the food served the tutor was much better than that served anyone else. Each time the servants brought in the food on trays, the youth and the tutor would look at each other and smile quietly together.

All good things are followed by bad, so the saying goes, and in the case of the tutor a matter of great concern arose.

After the silver spoon was found, the story of the tutor's magic powers spread throughout the house. It finally reached the ears of the head of the house.

Now, the young student's father, the master of the house, was a state minister in the king's court. Just at that time in the neighboring country of China, the

Chinese emperor lost his official seal. The whole
country was in a turmoil. Unless the emperor recovered his seal he would have to give up his throne
to another man.

All the fortunetellers and the soothsayers in China
were gathered together. Yet not one of them could
tell who had stolen this valuable seal. A messenger
was then sent to Korea who, after explaining the
situation to the king, asked: "Please send us your
very best soothsayer."

The king called his state ministers together to
consider who should be dispatched to China. One
of the ministers spoke up. It was the father of the
youth who had hidden the spoon.

"We have a tutor who just recently located the
whereabouts of a lost silver spoon. He is supposed
to be a very famous fortuneteller. What about sending this tutor of mine?"

"That's most fortunate."

"Let's follow your advice." The other ministers
of state all agreed to this suggestion.

The youth's father returned home and called the
tutor before him. "It will be a hard trip, but I would
like you to go to China on a mission," the minister
said, and then he told the tutor in detail the story

of the Chinese emperor's loss of his imperial seal.

"Oh, no! Not me. It's absurd!" the tutor said, and declined over and over again.

However, the minister had undertaken to send a soothsayer to China and he simply wouldn't take no for an answer. He was fully convinced the tutor was a great soothsayer. The greater a man, the more humble he is, the minister thought. Take this tutor for instance. Although he had the power to tell at one crack where the silver spoon had been hidden, not even once had he made known his ability. The tutor simply acted as any ordinary man would act. Thus, the minister was convinced that the tutor really was an extraordinary soothsayer.

"You don't have to be shy," the minister said. "Please do go. I beg you. There is nobody except you who can undertake this grave mission. Also, they say they will reward you with one hundred gold pieces. If you should succeed in finding the seal, imagine the honors that will be heaped upon you." In this way the minister finally forced upon the tutor the task of going to China whether he would or no.

The tutor did not care a thing about the reward of a hundred pieces of gold. But he could hardly bear the thought of the shame that would come to him when he was exposed. Of course, he thought, even if he could bear the shame, when they found out he had lied about his abilities, he would certainly be punished heavily.

"This is a terrible predicament," he thought, with pain in his heart. He went back to his room to ponder over the difficult position in which he found himself.

A few minutes later, his pupil came into his room, all smiles. "You needn't worry, tutor," he said. "This is what I would do." Then the young lad put his mouth to the tutor's ear and began whispering to him in a very low voice.

The tutor kept nodding his head and saying, "H'm, h'm." The worried expression on his face gradually disappeared, and suddenly a cheerful smile lit up his featurers.

The tutor did not reveal his plans to anyone. He completed his preparations and then departed with the emissary from the Chinese court. The two crossed the Yalu River and entered China. When they reached the Chinese capital, the tutor was ushered into the emperor's presence.

In a voice filled with confidence he told the emperor: "I shall find the seal for you within three months, so please put your mind at ease about it."

The emperor was very pleased and answered in a cheerful voice: "I cannot thank you enough." Then the emperor commanded that the tutor be treated with all due respect and his residence be closely guarded lest any mishap overtake him.

Two months soon passed for the tutor, who was living a life of luxury and splendor. Each morning he went through his act of telling fortunes and divining the whereabouts of the seal. One morning, after he had gone through this act, the tutor sighed with

great concern and murmured: "Oh, a terrible thing has happened."

Someone nearby who overheard his words asked: "What is the matter?"

"Oh, nothing to trouble you with. But last night a fire broke out in my house in Korea and burnt it to the ground. I don't care about the house, but the votive tablets of my ancestors were all destroyed too," the tutor answered, as if he had actually been at the scene of the fire.

"Can you tell such things too?" the person asked in surprise.

"Of course I can. If I couldn't tell such things, I wouldn't have come all this distance to look for the emperor's lost seal.'

The tutor's answer was so surprising that the person was filled with doubt. Even if the tutor were the best fortuneteller under the sun, he surely wouldn't be able to tell of a fire which happened thousands of miles away. And to say that the name-tables of his ancestors were also destroyed! How could anyone believe such a thing?

The person went straight to the emperor and told him of the incident. The emperor decided to send a messenger to Korea. The messenger was dispatched

ostensibly to pay the emperor's sympathies to the
tutor's family. But, actually, the emperor wanted to
find out for sure whether there had really been a fire
on that day.

After a while the messenger returned with the
report that there actually had been a fire on the very
day the tutor had said. In addition, the messenger
confirmed that the ancestral name-tablets had also
been lost, because the family had not been able to
get them out of the house quickly enough.

When this news got around, everyone in the
capital was deeply impressed. "The fortuneteller
from Korea is really a remarkable man...He even
knew of a fire that had taken place thousands of
miles away...That isn't all! Once that fortuneteller gets started, they say he can foretell events that
will take place a hundred years from now... Isn't he
a remarkable person? He is sure to find the emperor's
seal... They say he already knows who stole the
seal. Well, we can look forward to seeing the robber
executed soon...." Such tales spread quickly all
over the city, with embellishments added here and
there, until the capital buzzed with the supernatural
powers of the wizard from Korea.

The fire had actually been planned between the

tutor and his pupil long before. They had set a date
for the fire to take place, and the house had been set
afire on schedule. So there really was nothing to
marvel at. But the people of China, of course, did
not know this. They thought the tutor was a god
and treated him as if he were one.

As the stories of the tutor's prowess spread
throughout the country, the person most impressed
was naturally the man who had stolen the emperor's
seal. Not only was he impressed but also no little
worried. The tutor had said he would find the thief
within three months. The thief now felt that he
must do something quickly. He knew he would
be found out sooner or later, with the all-seeing eye
of the tutor reading into the hearts and souls of
everyone. So the thief said to himself: "If I am
to be found out eventually, I might as well give
myself up now and ask for mercy. In this way I
might at least save my life."

It was the next to the last day of the three-month
period the tutor had set for himself. A man slipped
fearfully into the tutor's room. He was the thief
who had stolen the emperor's seal. Making sure that
no one else was around, the thief bowed low before

the tutor and said: "Please spare my life."

His one eye flashing with anger, the tutor said: "You miserable fool! I was going to wait just one more day to see what you would do, and then I planned to go and tell the emperor your name. But now that you have come out and confessed your crime, I shall have pity on you and spare your life."

The thief was cowed by the solemn voice of the tutor, but with great relief he answered: "You will truly spare my life? Thank you from the bottom of my heart. The emperor's seal is hidden at the bottom of the pool in the middle of the Imperial Palace grounds."

"I knew that from before," the tutor said sternly. "I shall close my eyes to your crime this time, but you must never do such a thing again." The tutor then sent the man home.

Next day, the last of the three-month period, the tutor appeared before the emperor, who asked eagerly: "Have you discovered where the seal is hidden?"

The tutor answered: "Of course! Your worries are all over. I shall have it in your hands this very day. However, you must promise never to ask me who stole the seal. If you do, I will not be able to return the seal to you."

The emperor wanted the seal back so badly that he willingly agreed to the tutor's proposal.

"The seal is in the palace pool," the tutor said. "Please have the pool drained."

Immediately workers were set to work draining the pool. A thousand men busied themselves scooping out the water, and the bottom soon came into sight. And there the seal was!

Thus the seal was once again safe in the hands of the emperor. Thanks to the tutor, the entire country was freed from anxiety and fear. In addition to the promised hundred pieces of gold, the tutor was showered with many, many gifts.

His mission successfully completed, the tutor returned once more to Korea. There, his fame grew greater and greater than ever before. But his worries grew in proportion to his reputation. He could never tell when he would again be asked to tell fortunes or to divine secrets. Thus he was still in danger of being found out.

Once again, his pupil came up with a good idea. "Tell the people that you are sick, and stay out of sight for one month. After a month is over, tell them that you have recovered, but that because of your illness, you have lost all your powers of divination."

The tutor followed the youngster's suggestion and took to his bed. People kept coming from all over the country to ask for his help. But he refused to see any of them, saying that he was ill.

Then, blaming his illness, the tutor never again told any fortunes. As a result he was able to spend the rest of his life in peace, enjoying the great wealth he'd brought from China.

Other TUT BOOKS available:

TYPHOON! TYPHOON! An Illustrated Haiku Sequence *by Lucile M. Bogue*

UNBEATEN TRACKS IN JAPAN: An Account of Travels in the Interior Including Visits to the Aborigines of Yezo and the Shrine of Nikko *by Isabella L. Bird*

ZILCH! The Marine Corps' Most Guarded Secret *by Roy Delgado*

Please order from your bookstore or write directly to:

CHARLES E. TUTTLE CO., INC.
Suido 1-chome, 2–6, Bunkyo-ku, Tokyo 112

or:

CHARLES E. TUTTLE CO., INC.
Rutland, Vermont 05701 U.S.A.